365 Bedtime Duck Tales

text: Maike Karstkarel
illustrations: Maan Jansen

Backpack Books
122 Fifth Avenue
New York, NY 10011

ISBN 0-7607-7269-X

Printed and bound in Slovenia

05 06 07 08 09 MCH 10 9 8 7 6 5 4 3 2 1

Text: Maike Karstkarel
Illustrations: Maan Jansen
Cover design: AdAm Studio, Prague, The Czech Republic
Translation: Francesca Kudryashova for First Edition Translations Ltd, Cambridge,
          Great Britain
Typesetting: Cardinal Graphics for First Edition Translations Ltd, Cambridge,
          Great Britain
Prepress services: Amos Typographical Studio, Prague, The Czech Republic
Proofreading: Emily Sands, Eva Munk and Karen Taschek

365 Bedtime Duck Tales

text: Maike Karstkarel
illustrations: Maan Jansen

BACK**PACK**BOOKS
◦
NEW YORK

January 1

A new year

Simon Duckling is looking a bit sleepy.
Can you see him yawning? He went to bed very late last night.
Do you know why? Simon was at a party.
He was at a party with all the other ducks on the pond.
The food was delicious and they all enjoyed themselves.
The party ended with a firework show.
The ducks were celebrating the end of the old year and the beginning of
a new year. The new year has already begun. Today is the first day of the
new year. A year full of exciting and fun adventures about large ducks,
small ducks, white, green and brown ducks, real ducks and toy ducks too.
In short, lots of stories about ducks. Simon is looking forward to hearing
about the next day's adventures, but he needs to go to sleep now, because
he can hardly keep his eyes open. He puts his head under his wing.
Do you want to hear all about the adventures too?
Or are you a bit too sleepy like Simon?

Cutting out ducks

Thomas and Sally are sitting at the kitchen table. They are a bit bored. Mother comes into the room. "You two look miserable," she says, "what's the matter?" "We can't think of anything to play," says Thomas. "We can't go outside either, because it's raining," adds Sally. Mother thinks for a minute. Then she says: "Wait a minute, I've an idea." She goes out of the kitchen and returns with a pile of colored paper and three pairs of scissors. "Watch carefully," she says. She picks up the scissors and begins to cut something out of a piece of paper. Thomas and Sally look at Mother with surprise. What is she doing? There, Mother has finished. Look, she has cut out a lovely little duck. "I can do that too," says Thomas, and takes a piece of paper. Sally joins in. So the three of them sit and cut out lots of lovely colored paper ducks. When they have finished, Thomas and Sally stick the ducks on a large sheet of paper and draw water and flowers around them. When the whole thing is finished, they put the picture on the wall so that everyone can see it. Isn't it lovely?

January 3

Good friends

Freddy and Mandy Duckling are good friends. They are always together.
They like playing tag down by the pond best, or playing with a ball. But when it is
cold, they stay inside and read comics together. They are at Mandy's house today.
It is half past five, nearly time for supper for ducklings. Freddy is invited to supper,
because Mandy's father is making pancakes! He is making two sorts of pancakes:
pancakes with apple and pancakes with bacon. Freddy and Mandy are allowed to
put as much syrup on the pancakes as they wish. Yummy! After their pancakes,
Mandy's mother gives them both a cup of chocolate milk. Then it is
time for Freddy to go home, because it is almost bedtime.

January 4

The lost beak

Listen here! Listen!
To what I'm telling you.
The duck has lost his beak.
Whatever shall he do?

Wherever has it gone?
He's such a silly duck.
If he looks down, he might
Just find it in the muck.

I have it, I've got it, I've found it.
I'll jump up in the air,
Splash into the river,
Quack, quack, I don't care!

Funny gloves

Look, here comes Sam. Has he got warm clothes on? He needs them, because it is cold outside. Sam is waving. But what are those on his hands? Aren't they funny things? They look a bit like ducks. They are greenish with a red thing that looks a bit like a beak. Let's take a closer look. Yes, now I can see! They're gloves. Knitted duck gloves. Don't they look funny!

January 6

A sweater with a duck

Grandma is sitting on a chair by the window. She is knitting a sweater for Jenny.
Not just an ordinary sweater. No, she's knitting a sweater with a duck on it.
A big, yellow duck. A duck with a red beak and orange legs. And Grandma gives him a blue hat just for fun. There, the sweater is finished. Jenny has to try it on, of course. It fits perfectly. Doesn't it look lovely?

January 7

Catching snowflakes

Robbie and Eric Duckling are playing by the duck pond.
All of a sudden it begins to snow. Big, fat snowflakes fall from the sky.
"Oh, look," calls out Robbie, "look at the big snowflakes."
They look up at the sky together. "I know a good game to play with snow,"
says Eric. "Catch snowflakes in your beak. Whoever catches
the most is the winner." Robbie and Eric open their beaks
and try to catch as many snowflakes as they can.
"I've got ten!" shouts Eric. "Let's see," says Robbie. Eric opens his beak.
"I can't see anything at all," says Robbie. "I think they melted."
Hmm, Eric hadn't thought of that. "But I really did catch ten," he says.
They continue with their game and try to catch
lots and lots more snowflakes.

My feet are stuck!

Everything is frozen hard. There is a thick layer of ice on the duck pond. Victor Duckling is walking on it. He stops walking and stands still. He is looking at the pond. It is so pretty and white with snow. Then he tries to keep walking, but he can't move. His feet are stuck. He tries to pull them free, but they remain firmly stuck to the ice. He pulls a bit harder, but that doesn't work either. Whatever shall he do? Victor begins to shout very loudly. "Help," he shouts. "Help, my feet are stuck!" Has anyone heard him? Yes, someone has. John, the elderly duck who lives in a house close to the pond, has heard Victor shouting. John rushes to Victor's rescue with a kettle of warm water. He pours the warm water onto the ice. And look, Victor's feet are free. Victor gets off the ice as quickly as he can. What a fright he had! He decides to play inside for the rest of the day.

January 9

Feeding the ducks

Lisa and her mother are going to the park.
They are taking a large bag of bread.
The bread is for the ducks in the park. There is
often snow on the ground in the winter so the
ducks can't find very much food. This is
why Lisa is bringing them food.
There are lots of ducks on the pond. Lisa
throws some bits of bread down on the ground.
The ducks are quick to notice the food.
Mmm, they really enjoy it. When all the
bread is finished, Lisa goes home.
Good-bye, ducks. See you next time!

January 10

Frank is ill

Frank is in bed. He is ill and coughs
all the time. He has just seen the doctor,
who brought a large bag full
of things. One of the things
in his bag was for listening.
The doctor put one part in his ears
and the other on Frank's back.
Brr, that was cold. Frank had to take
a deep breath so that the doctor could
hear properly. Then the doctor said that
Frank had the flu and must stay in bed.
Frank also got some cough medicine.
Frank doesn't feel very happy, but he
snuggles down in bed with his cuddly
duck. He'll be better soon, won't he?

January 11

Making a snow duck

There is ice on the pond and it is snowing. Mandy and Freddy Duckling
are really excited. What shall they do? Go sleding or throw snowballs?
"I know!" shouts Freddy. "Let's make a snowman!"
They begin right away. They make a snowman that looks just like
Father Duck. They use big, black buttons for the eyes, and half a
carrot for his beak. There! It's finished. A snow white Father Duck
stands proudly in the garden. Doesn't he look nice?

January 12

When it freezes

Hip, hip, hurray! The pond is covered with ice.
Ssh, don't tell the ducks because it isn't nice for them.
When children go skating on the frozen pond,
The ducks quack wildly, for they are not fond
Of ice since they can swim no more
Until the ice melts into water as before.

The ice slide

There is a hard frost. The duck pond has frozen. Gus and Flappy Duckling are trying out the ice to see if it holds. Gus puts one foot very carefully on the ice. It doesn't creak. Then Flappy steps onto the ice too. But oh dear, Flappy slips and falls over. Boom! Flappy falls flat on his bottom. The ice is really slippery! Gus bursts out laughing. Flappy is lucky and hasn't hurt himself. He quite enjoyed his slide on the ice! So they slide on the ice together, from one side of the pond, swoosh, to the other. What a good game!

Sledding together

"Now it's my turn," calls out Tim Duckling to his friend Tom. Tim and Tom are playing outside with the sled in the snow. They are taking turns sledding down a high hill. Tim climbs up the hill. Swoosh! He sleds down at top speed. "I'll take another turn," says Tim. "No," says Tom, "now it's my turn." They nearly begin to argue. Then Tim says: "I know. We'll go together." So they both climb up the hill. At the top, they sit on the sled together and…swoosh, there they go! Sledding together is much more fun than on your own!

Grandpa Duck

Grandpa Duck is very old and very friendly.
He wears a striped purple suit and a smart
red tie. He generally sits in an easy chair
by the window. He likes to wave at all the
ducklings playing outside by the pond.
When he goes out, he puts on a black
top hat and twirls his walking stick.
Hello, Grandpa Duck!

January 16

Visiting Grandpa Duck

Tim is going to visit Grandpa Duck.
He loves going to visit Grandpa.
Grandpa tells him stories about long ago and
lets him look at his big photograph album.
There are photographs of all the Duck family
in this album. Uncle and Aunt Duck are
there. So are all Tim's cousins. And of course,
there is a photograph of Tim too, when
he was still only a tiny duckling.
Grandpa gives Tim some chocolate to eat
and a glass of lemonade to drink. Tim gives
Grandpa a big hug when it is time to leave.
See you next time, Grandpa Duck!

January 17

That's clever!

Wobble Duckling is walking across the duck pond. The duck pond is frozen, so he can walk on it. Wobble hears his tummy rumbling. He is hungry. Wobble would really like a nice fish to eat. But all the fish are under the ice. He can't reach them. But he has an idea. He finds a stick and pokes a hole in the ice with it. Then he goes and gets his fishing rod, puts some bread on the hook, and lowers the hook through the hole into the water. Isn't that clever? Let's just hope Wobble catches a fish.

January 18

Turning circles

Watch out, watch out,
I'm learning to skate
And sliding all over.
Oh, isn't it great!

I skate to the right,
It's the easiest thing.
I skate to the left,
Watch me skate in a ring.

With both feet together,
Turning quickly around.
Sometimes it goes wrong
And I fall on the ground.

A difficult jigsaw puzzle

Jeremy is sitting at the kitchen table.
He is doing a jigsaw puzzle. It has
a hundred pieces. Jeremy's mother
wanted to help, but Jeremy didn't
want her to. He wanted to do it all
by himself. He has already put all
the edge pieces together. He still has
to put the middle pieces in.
You can already see what it is going
to be. There is sky at the top and
grass at the bottom. There are things
with beaks in the picture. Do you
think you can guess what they are?

January 20

Making animal noises

Maggie and Will are playing a game. Maggie makes an animal noise and Will has to
guess which animal it is. "Meow," says Maggie. "That's easy," says Will, "that's a cat."
"Correct," says Maggie. "Now it's your turn." "Woof, woof," says Will.
"I know," says Maggie, "that's a dog. I've got another one. Squeak, squeak."
Will has to think. Yes, he's got it. "It's a mouse," he says.
"Right again," says Maggie. "Now it's your turn again."
"Quack," says Will. Maggie thinks hard, but she can't guess.
Do you know which animal it is?

January 21

Nearly tummy ache

Ricky Duckling is visiting Aunt Duck with his mother. It is Aunt's birthday. Ricky isn't really enjoying himself, because all the others are grown-up ducks. And all they do is talk. There are some nice duck snacks on the table: a big fish pie and duckweed tea. Ricky tries a piece of the pie. Nobody is paying any attention to him. Mmm, delicious. He takes another piece, and another…. He eats so much pie that he nearly gets a tummy ache. Nobody notices. The big ducks are just so busy talking!

January 22

The diary

Fiona Duckling has a diary with a lock on it. Nobody is allowed to read it. Fiona is still a bit too small to be able to write, but she is very good at drawing. Each evening she draws a picture in her diary of what has happened that day. Today she has drawn her friend Elsa and a ball, because they played ball together. There are already lots of drawings in the diary. Luckily there are lots more pages too, so Fiona can do lots more drawings.

January 23

Dressing up as Mother

Clara Duckling is upstairs. She is in
Mother and Father Duck's bedroom.
She is playing dress up. She has put on one
of Mother's dresses and a pair of her shoes.
They are beautiful shoes with high heels.
She has found a pretty necklace too.
She almost looks like Mother.
She just needs a bit of makeup,
some lipstick and a dash of eye shadow,
and there she is! Finished!
Doesn't she look beautiful?

January 24

Muscles

Oh what a funny sight to see.
He works out all day long.
A duck who's lifting weights all day
I think will be quite strong.

Look at the bulging muscles.
(Even on his nose!)
Look out, don't drop those weights,
Or you'll have some bulging toes!

The high tower

Jasper has been given a box of blocks. It is a big box of blocks with lots of blocks inside. There are square blocks and rectangular blocks. Some blocks are very big, others are small. Jasper builds a tower with the blocks, a high tower. A tower almost as tall as Jasper himself. Gertie, Jasper's toy duck, is watching. Gosh, the tower is very high. I hope it doesn't topple over!

January 26

A house for Gertie

Jasper is in the living room. He is playing with his blocks. He isn't building a tower. No, he's building a house. Do you know who for? Jasper is making a house for Gertie, his toy duck. The house is nearly finished. The walls are done and so is the door. It just needs a roof. There, finished! Gertie is very pleased with her new house. It is just her size.

The toy duck

Peace at last, thought the little duck. He was floating gently in the bath.
He had been played with all evening. He had been thrown about and pushed
underwater. Now all the children had had their baths and he could rest.
Flipper, for that was the duck's name, didn't really like being a toy duck.
He would have much preferred to be a real duck. Then he could have swum
in the pond and nobody would have played with him so roughly.
Oh well, that's life, he supposed. At least he could dream about
being a real duck now that he had been left in peace.
But do you really think the life of a real duck
is as much fun as Flipper thinks?

An unusual duck

This is Tanya Duckling. She has beautiful, colorful feathers. Tanya is no ordinary duckling. No, she comes from a country far, far away. The ducks look very different where she comes from. This is why Tanya is so beautiful. I'd love to have a suit of lovely colored feathers like Tanya's, wouldn't you?

January 29

The duckling from Sweden

In Sweden long ago,
A foolish duck said:
"Oh! How silly of me,
I've swallowed a pea."
The pea lay quite still
So the duck wasn't ill.
It wasn't so bad.
In fact, he was glad!
Then it started to grow
(Peas grow upward, you know.)
You could tell, so they said,
By the leaves on his head.

Special cakes

Mother is in the kitchen. She is making cakes and Joseph is allowed to help. Mother isn't making ordinary cakes – she's making special ones.
First she makes the mix. She puts flour in a bowl, then adds butter, some sugar, and two eggs. Joseph mixes everything together and beats it until it is ready.
Joseph is wearing a large apron to keep him clean. When the mixture is ready, they roll it into small balls. Then they flatten the balls on the kitchen table. Then comes the best bit. Mother has a duck-shaped cutter. She cuts the mixture into duck shapes. When she has finished, she gives the duck shapes to Joseph. He puts a raisin in for an eye. The ducks look almost as if they're real. Then it is time to put the duck cakes in the oven. Mmm, that smells good. I bet the duck cakes will taste good, too. What do you think?

January 31

Felt pen everywhere

Henry has to look after his little brother
Dick this afternoon. Mother has gone shopping
and Henry has to stay at home with Dick.
"I know," says Henry, "let's do a drawing."
Dick thinks it's a good idea. Henry gets out a big box
of felt pens and some paper. They sit on the floor side
by side. Henry does a lovely drawing of a duck surrounded
by ducklings. "Look what I've drawn," he says, showing
his drawing to his little brother. But
where is Dick? He's not sitting next to him on the
floor anymore. Henry looks around the room.
Oh no! Dick is doing a drawing, but on the wall!
Felt pen everywhere! The whole wall is covered
in felt pen. Mother will not be pleased.
Henry takes the pen away from Dick and says:
"You mustn't draw on the walls. You must draw
on the paper." Dick looks a bit puzzled.
He had done such a lovely drawing.
They quickly wipe the wall clean
so that Mother won't notice.
Then they keep drawing.
But this time on the paper!

February 1

At the fair

Jacob is at the fair with his father. There are lots of things to see. There is a merry-go-round and a shooting gallery, and lots of other games to play. Jacob has been on the merry-go-round. Now he wants to try the tin can game.

There are five tin cans on a shelf, and Jacob must try to knock them off with a ball. The fairground lady gives him three balls. Jacob throws one of the balls as hard as he can. Crash! Two tin cans fall to the ground. Three left. Jacob throws again. Yes, he's knocked down two more. Just one tin can left. Jacob throws his last ball and…yes, the last tin can is knocked off the shelf.

Jacob may choose a prize as he has knocked down all the tin cans. He chooses a lovely, big, cuddly duck. What a good prize!

Building a den

Ivan and Nick Duckling are playing outside by the pond. They are building a den. Ivan and Nick have collected lots of rushes. These are the walls of the den, and the floor is going to be covered with moss. It will be nice and soft to sit on. The den is nearly finished. It just needs a roof. They make the roof of large leaves. There, it's finished. The den is just big enough for the two of them. Now Ivan and Nick have their own little house!

February 3

Hide-and-seek

Dick and Gerry Duckling are playing outside. They are playing hide-and-seek. Gerry is counting to ten with his eyes closed. Dick runs away and hides. When Gerry has finished counting, he opens his eyes and looks around. Where is Dick hiding? Gerry looks behind a tree. No Dick. He's not in the bushes either. But wait a minute, why is that bush moving? Look, you can just see the tip of Dick's tail sticking out. Found you!
Now it's Gerry's turn to hide.

February 4

Where is Gus?

"Gus, time for supper," calls Mother Duck.
But Gus Duckling doesn't appear. Mother calls again.
Still no Gus. Wherever could he be?
She looks in the living room and in the hall.
Gus is nowhere to be seen. Mother goes back to the kitchen.
Just a minute, who's that under the kitchen table?
You guessed…it is Gus!

February 5

A strange duck

Somewhere in France,
Near Fayence,
Lived a strange and
Silly duck.

He wore his hose
And other clothes
All front to back –
Silly quack!

A frog

Harold Duckling is walking around the
edge of the pond. Suddenly something moves
in the water. Someone pops his head out
of the water. "Croak," he says.
"Quack," says Harold, surprised.
"You don't look very much like a duck,
but you sound very like one."
"Croak," he says again. "Of course
I'm not a duck, silly, I'm a frog."
"Oh," says Harold. "Then, hello, Mr. Frog."
"Hello and good-bye," croaks the frog, and
jumps back into the water.

February 7

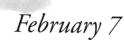

A competition

Wobble is playing with his duckling friend,
Tom. They are playing with a go-cart.
"Let's have a competition," says Wobble,
"from here to the tree over there.
Whoever gets there first wins."
Tom thinks it's a good idea.
"Ready, steady," says Wobble, "go!"
There they go. They pedal as fast as they
can. Tom pedals just that bit faster
than Wobble. He gets to the tree first.
"Hurray, I've won!" shouts Tom. Then
they race again so that Wobble can have
another chance to win.

February 8

The duck chorus

Can you see all those ducks standing in a group over there? That is the duck chorus. You are only allowed to join if you quack most beautifully. There are some ducks in the chorus who can quack very high, and others who can quack very low. Together they try to sing a lovely duck song. At the moment, however, it just sounds like a lot of noise. They need to practice a lot to make it sound better. They will all have to try very hard.

February 9

Beware of the cat!

A little duckling is scratching about at the edge of the pond. He is looking for food. But what's that sitting behind the tree? Oh dear, it's the cat. The cat is hungry too. She creeps quietly up to the duckling. The duckling does not see the cat. Sweet little duckling, do be careful, because here comes the cat! The cat creeps closer to the duckling. She is just ready to pounce when the duckling jumps into the water and swims away. Just in time!

The neighbor

Now listen, now listen,
Believe what you hear
About my new neighbor
Who lives very near.

She found seven eggs,
And hatched them all out.
Now she has seven ducklings
All running about.

To the hairdresser's

Frank has to go to the hairdresser's.
He doesn't want to go.
He hates having his hair cut.
He doesn't like the hairdresser fiddling
with his hair. And it itches too.
But Frank's mother has said that
he has to go. Frank is cross and sad
at the same time. Then his mother
has a good idea. Frank can take his
cuddly duck with him to the
hairdresser's, and he can sit on
Frank's knee while his hair is being cut.
Frank will feel much better then.

February 12

Soaking wet

It has been raining hard. There are puddles all around the
edge of the duck pond. Otto and William Duckling are
a bit bored. They walk around the puddles. Then Otto
accidentally steps in a puddle. His foot now is soaking wet.
"Ha ha," laughs William, "you've got a wet foot."
"Just you wait," says Otto, and stamps his foot in the
puddle. The water splashes everywhere. All over William.
"I can do that too," says William, and stamps his own foot
in the puddle. The water splashes everywhere again. All
over Otto. Otto is wet from head to toe. But he doesn't
mind. He thinks it's funny. He jumps right in
the middle of the puddle, as hard as he can.
The water splashes much higher and makes them both wet
all over. Then they both jump from one puddle to another
until they are so wet they can't get any wetter. What an
excellent game for ducklings!

The coloring-in picture

Benny is coloring. He was given a very nice picture to color.
It is a picture of a duck. The duck is still completely white.
But it won't stay that way for long because Benny is going to color it in with
his crayons. It is going to be a man duck, a drake. Benny colors the head green
and the wings gray and brown. He gives it an orange beak and orange legs.
There, the duck is finished. Well done, Benny!

February 14

A lovely bandage

Look, there's Peter on his new bicycle.
He's very good at biking. But he's not
looking where he's going. Boom! He falls
on his knee with a crash. It hurts, and Peter
starts to cry. He runs home to his mother,
and shows her his cut knee.
Mother knows what to do. She fetches
a big Band-Aid, not just an ordinary
Band-Aid, but one with a picture of ducks
on it. She sticks the bandage onto his
sore knee. Then she gives it a gentle kiss,
just to be sure. Don't worry, Peter,
your knee will be better soon.

February 15

A worm

Mandy and Freddy Duckling are playing outside.
It has just stopped raining and the ground is still wet.
"Eek!" shrieks Mandy. "What is that horrible thing?"
She points at the ground. A thin, wriggly thing is poking
its way out of the ground. Freddy begins to laugh.
"Why are you laughing?" says Mandy crossly.
"It isn't a bit funny. I think it's frightening!"
"Oh, come on, it's only a worm," says Freddy.
"You don't need to be afraid of a worm. He won't bite,
you know. All he does is dig tunnels under the ground.
It helps the plants to grow, which is a good thing.
You can catch fish with them, too."
Mandy is still a bit wary of the worm. She won't go
anywhere near it. She just thinks it looks horrible.

February 16

Raining mud!

It has been raining. The duck pond is surrounded by deep puddles.
Joshua and Boris Duckling are walking around the outside of the puddles.
Then Joshua dips one of his wings into a puddle. He swishes his feathers
around in the mud. He scoops up a wingful of mud and throws it into the air.
Oh dear, his aim wasn't very good because the mud falls all over Boris.
Boris gets a bit of a fright, but begins to laugh.
"I can do that too!" he says, and scoops up a wingful of mud, just like
Joshua. He throws it high into the air. Both Joshua and Boris get
covered in mud, but they don't mind one bit. They think making
mud rain is fun. Later they'll go for a swim, dive into the
water and wash all the mud from their feathers.

Too small trousers

Now listen to me,
And my little song
About a duck from Bristol
Whose trousers were all wrong.

First they were too big,
So they cut the legs short.
Now they're far too small.
He looks silly!

February 18

Chocolate everywhere!

Hugo Duckling is sitting at the kitchen table. He is making himself a sandwich.
First he spreads butter on the bread. Then he picks up the jar of chocolate chips.
He gives the jar a shake. Hey, that makes a nice sound. Hugo dances around the table
shaking the chocolate chip jar and singing. But oh dear, all of a sudden…flop!
The top flies off the jar. And all the chocolate chips fly all over the kitchen.
Hugo thinks it's very funny. There are chocolate chips everywhere.
It may be funny, but Hugo is a bit worried about what Mother will say.
So he quickly cleans it all up. He hopes Mother won't notice.

Blowing bubbles

Herman and Jasper Duckling are playing outside. Do you know what they are doing? They are blowing bubbles. They both have a cup of soapy water and a stick. A stick with a circle at one end. Herman dips his stick into the cup, so that some soap suds get caught in the circle. Then Herman blows gently through the circle. Look! Lots of bubbles appear. They float up into the sky. It is a lovely sight. Some of the bubbles are big, but others are small. Jasper blows too, very carefully, and makes a great big bubble. It gleams with lots of pretty colors. And it floats so high! Jasper and Herman keep on blowing lots more bubbles. It looks as if the sky is full of them!

February 20

Always together

Sarah has a cuddly duck. He is called Kwacky and is lovely and soft. Sarah takes Kwacky everywhere with her. She takes him visiting and when she goes shopping. She never leaves Kwacky behind. Even when she goes to school, she takes him with her. Sometimes she just holds him, but sometimes she puts him inside her jacket. They really are always together. And when it's time for bed, Kwacky is there beside Sarah in her bed. Snuggled close. Night night, Sarah. Night night, Kwacky.

February 21

The silly duck

There once was a duck
Who lived in a nest.
He did silly things,
Quite unlike the rest.

He painted his feet
Ten colors, they say.
Then he lay down and counted
Grass blades all through the day.

He stood on his head,
Blew bubbles for luck.
I never have seen
Such a silly old duck!

February 22

A big fish

Tim and Tom Duckling are sitting at the edge of the pond fishing.
They both have a fishing rod with a line. Very near to the end of the line is a float
bobbing about on the water. There is a piece of bread on the hook underneath the
float. When the float begins to bob up and down, it means that there is probably a fish
on the hook.
Fish like bread. "Have you got a bite?" asks Tom.
"No," replies Tim, "my float isn't moving at all."
"Neither is mine," says Tom. But at that moment his float begins to bob about wildly.
Tom pulls in his line, but he can hardly hold it. Tim comes to help. They pull on the
fishing rod together. There is a big fish on the end of the line. When the fish is nearly
out of the water, the line breaks. Tim and Tom fall backward onto their bottoms.
And the fish? The fish swims away as quick as it can.

February 23

A lovely present

Josie has been given something very nice.
She is very happy with her present. Do you
know what it is? It is a badge. A badge with
a duck on it. It is a very sweet duck and looks
very smart indeed. Josie has put on her
red sweater today specially, because the
badge will look very good on it.
Josie is very proud of her duck badge.

February 24

On the train

Lisa is going on a train journey with her mother and father. They are going to visit
Grandma, and Lisa's cuddly duck is going, too. Lisa and her duck are sitting by the
window so that they can see everything. They see big fields with cows and sheep.
Then they see houses, and look, there's a windmill! A man in a uniform comes along
to check their tickets. Duck hasn't got a ticket, but the man says ducks may travel free.
Here they are! The train has arrived. Grandma is waiting on the platform.
Lisa enjoyed the trip on the train and she's fairly sure that Duck enjoyed it too.

February 25

The ball is stuck

Mandy and Freddy Duckling are playing
in the water. They are playing a game with a ball.
"I can throw much higher than you," says Freddy.
"Prove it," says Mandy. Freddy throws the
ball up high with his beak.
"Is that all? I can easily throw as high as that,"
says Mandy. She throws the ball high into the
air with her beak. So very high that the ball gets
stuck in the tree between two branches. They can't
reach it. "I have an idea," says Freddy. "We'll shake
the tree until the ball just falls out." They climb out
of the water and go over to the tree. They shake the
tree as hard as they can. Look, it's worked. The ball
falls to the ground, and Mandy and Freddy can
continue with their game, far away from the tree.

February 26

A special doll's house

Josephine is in her bedroom. She is playing with her doll's house. It is a very special doll's house. It should really be called a duck's house, because tiny ducks live in it, not dolls. There is a Father Duck, a Mother Duck, and seven Duck children. It is a very big house, so they all fit in easily. There is a kitchen and a sitting room, and some tiny chairs and a tiny table in the sitting room. It even has real curtains. The house also has an attic, and a swing and a seesaw outside for the duck children to play on. Josephine thinks the house is lovely. In fact, she'd quite like to live in it herself.

February 27

A question

I know a duckling
Who is all alone.
He's no friends at all,
Nor does he have a home.

So I have a question,
Please answer me true.
May this lonely duckling
Come and live with you?

February 28

The duck in the book

Victor is sitting on the sofa.
He is reading a book
about a duck. There are lovely pictures
in the book. The duck has lots of
exciting adventures and travels to lots
of distant countries. He meets a great
many animals. A cow, a sheep, an
elephant, a giraffe, and even a crocodile.
Victor would like to change places with
that duck. Then he would be able to have
exciting adventures, just like the duck
in the book. Wouldn't that be fun!

March 1

Brushing teeth

Yuri is in the bathroom with his cuddly duck. He's on his way to bed.
But first he must brush his teeth. Mother is helping him. She puts the
toothpaste on Yuri's toothbrush, then they brush together. Yuri brushes
his teeth very well because he doesn't want to get any cavities in them.
When he has finished, he rinses his mouth with water.
"Duck needs to brush his teeth too," says Yuri.
He puts some toothpaste on the toothbrush. But, wait a minute,
Duck hasn't got any teeth. So he doesn't need to brush them.
Isn't that easy? Yuri goes to bed. So does Duck. Night night, Yuri.
See you in the morning!

A ladybird

"Just look at that," says Mandy Duckling to Freddy Duckling. "Look, what is on that flower?" "That's a ladybug," says Freddy. "Why are there spots on its back?" asks Mandy. Freddy thinks for a moment, then says: "So you can tell how old it is." Maggie counts the spots. "One, two, three, four. That means he's four years old. I think that's a bit strange, because I'm four, too, but I haven't any spots on my back." "But you're not a ladybug," laughs Freddy. Mandy doesn't know whether to believe Freddy or not. Do you think Freddy is right?

March 3

The duck from Ryde

There once was a duck
Who lived in Ryde.
Guess what? His beak
Grew out at one side.

The side, not the front,
And I tell you no lies –
For I saw it myself
With my very own eyes.

The angry neighbor

"Kick the ball," shouts Rick Duckling to
Paul Duckling. Paul kicks the ball to Rick.
They are playing soccer together outside.
"Here it comes," shouts Rick, and gives
the ball a really hard kick. Oh dear!
The ball goes the wrong way. It lands
in the neighbor's garden.
"I'm not getting it," says Paul.
"Nor am I," says Rick. But he creeps
carefully into the neighbor's garden.
Just as he picks up the ball he hears an
angry voice. "Who's that in my garden?
Get out, you horrible boy!"
It's the neighbor, and he is rather cross.
Rick runs out of the garden as quickly as
he can. "Come on, Paul, run!" he shouts,
and they both run away as fast as their
legs will take them. When they get around
the corner they stop, out of breath.
That was just in time, wasn't it!

March 5

A special bank

Derek has a new bank. It is a duck. Not a real duck, of course, but a duck made of china. The duck is very big. You can put lots of money in it. There is a slit in the top of the duck. This is where Derek puts the money in. When Derek has saved lots of money, he is going to buy something he wants. He hasn't decided what he's going to buy, yet. He's still thinking about it. That doesn't matter, though, because the bank isn't full yet.

March 6

The rocking duck

Thomas's little brother has been given a rocking duck. You've heard of a rocking horse? Well, this is a rocking duck. Thomas's brother can sit on it and rock to and fro. He loves it. Thomas is really far too big for the rocking duck, but sometimes, when nobody is looking, he climbs on the duck and has a little rock. But don't tell anyone!

Paddle boats

Ronny and Donny Duckling are playing on the pond. They are playing on paddle boats, which are a bit like regular boats, but there are pedals in them, just like on a bicycle. When the pedals go around, the paddle boat goes forward. Ronny and Donny are a bit tired after all that pedaling. They stop for a while, right in the middle of the pond in the sunshine. They'll continue in a minute.

March 8

What big ducks!

"Aren't they big ducks?" says Tim Duckling with surprise. He's having a swim
in the pond with his mother. "Look at their big wings," says Tim,
"and their necks are really long. They're white, too." Tim's mother laughs.
"They're not ducks, silly," she says, "they're swans!"
"Swans?" says Tim, "I've never heard of swans."
"Yes, swans," says Mother. "They look a bit like ducks, but they're much bigger
and they are a different color." Tim now knows that swans and ducks are different.

March 9

Sandcastles

There once was a duck
Who lived by the sea.
He built giant sandcastles
For all to see.

With very high towers
And water all around.
No finer castles
Will ever be found.

March 10

New pants

Gerry Duckling is in town with his mother. He needs new pants. If there's one thing that Gerry hates, it's buying new pants. Gerry doesn't mind having new clothes; it's having to try them on in a changing room that he hates. It's always the same. One pair of pants is too big, another is too small. Sometimes you have to try on lots of pairs until you find a pair that fits. This time Gerry is lucky. He finds a pair that fits him almost right away. Then he and Mother go to a café for a glass of lemonade and some cake. Now that part Gerry does like!

March 11

Harriet writes a letter

Harriet Duckling is sitting at the kitchen table. She is writing a letter.
A letter to Grandma and Grandpa. Do you know what she has written?
"Dear Grandma and Grandpa, please may I come to stay with you soon?
I really like it at your house. Love from Harriet."
Harriet puts the letter in an envelope. Mother puts a stamp on it before
it is mailed. Harriet hopes that the letter doesn't get lost in the mail.

March 12

Paint

Ronald Duckling is sitting at the table. He is painting with finger paints.
Ronald is doing his very best painting and is concentrating so hard that he
doesn't notice his clothes brushing the paint. Mother Duck comes into the room.
"What have you been doing?" she asks. "I've been painting," says Ronald.
"Just look at your clothes," says Mother. Ronald looks down and sees the paint on
his clothes. Paint marks everywhere. He's lucky that Mother isn't mad. She fetches one
of Father's old shirts. Ronald puts it on. It doesn't matter if an old shirt gets covered
in paint so Ronald keeps finger painting quite happily.

A dressing-up party

Mandy and Freddy Duckling are playing up in the attic. There is a big, old trunk up there full of old clothes. Mandy and Freddy decide to play dress up. Mandy puts on a long dress and shoes with high heels. The shoes are really too big and wobble a bit, but it doesn't matter. Freddy puts on a suit. And a tie, but it's quite tricky to knot the tie. Then they both put on a hat. "Ha ha," laughs Mandy, "you do look funny!" "You should look at yourself!" says Freddy. They stand in front of a mirror together. They laugh so much that their tummies begin to hurt. Don't they look funny in those old clothes?

March 14

Eva's cuddly duckling

Eva has a cuddly duckling that she loves very much. Her duckling is called Squeak. It is a sweet little thing with a red beak. When Eva goes outside to play with her friends, she always sits Squeak on her big, soft teddy bear's lap. Then Squeak won't be lonely. And Teddy has company too!

March 15

Where is Squeak?

Eva is very sad. She can't find Squeak. He's just disappeared. Do you think Squeak has run away? She looks everywhere. In the cupboard, on top of the cupboard, in the drawer, in the basket. Squeak is nowhere to be found. Father and Mother look for Squeak…but nobody can find him. Where could he be?

March 16

Squeak

Eva looks in every corner,
Looking for duckling Squeak.

Little duck, wherever are you?
Please come back to me this week.

Eva cannot find her duckling.
Someone, please find Squeak!

March 17

Under the bed

It is time for Eva to go to bed. Of course she won't be able to go to sleep without Squeak, her cuddly duckling. She begins to cry.
Mother tells her an extra-long story to cheer her up, but Eva is still sad.
But what's that? thinks Mother. What's that under the bed? Could it be Squeak? Yes, it is! What a relief! Eva falls asleep right away, cuddling Squeak tight in her arms. She doesn't want him to escape again.

March 18

Secret duck language

Megan and Penny Duckling are sitting on the sofa in the living room.
"I know a good game," says Penny. "Let's invent a secret duck language."
"Secret duck language?" says Megan, surprised. "What's that?"
"Oh, it's easy," says Penny. "Each word we say must begin with
the letter *m*. Not how are you, but mow mare mou?"
"Oh, I see," says Megan. "So I wouldn't say I'm fine,
thank you. I'd say mi'm mine, mank mou."
"Yes," says Penny, "you've got it." Mother Duck comes into the room.
"Hello," she says. "Mello," reply Penny and Megan.
"I beg your pardon?" says Mother.
"Mello, Mother, me maid," say Megan and Penny.
Mother doesn't understand a word. But we do, don't we?

March 19

A letter from Grandpa and Grandma Duck

Harriet Duckling goes to the mailbox. There might be a letter for her in it.
Yes, there is. It is from Grandpa and Grandma. Do you know what it says?
"Dear Harriet, please come and stay with us soon. We would like that very much.
Love from Grandpa and Grandma." Harriet is very happy with her letter. She is so
pleased that she is invited to stay at Grandpa and Grandma's. She can hardly wait.

March 20

Away visiting

Harriet Duckling is going to stay with Grandpa and
Grandma. She and Mother packed her bag together.
They packed her pajamas, a toothbrush, and some extra
clothes. Father Duck is taking her there in the car.
It's quite a long drive. Grandpa and Grandma are waiting
for Harriet to arrive. They are very excited.
"Good-bye, Harriet," says Father, "see you in a
couple of days. I'll come and get you."
"Good-bye," says Harriet, and waves as
Father drives off home. Good-bye!

Spring

Today is a special day. Today is the first day of spring. The sun shines in the spring and flowers begin to grow. Lots of baby animals are born in the spring too. Cows have calves, sheep have lambs – sometimes two at once. Then they are twins. Horses have foals. But what about the birds? Birds lay their eggs in the spring. Tiny baby birds hatch out of the eggs. Ducks lay eggs too. The duck sits on the eggs for a long time to keep them warm. After a while, the eggs hatch and baby ducks come out of the shells. What a lot of interesting things happen in spring!

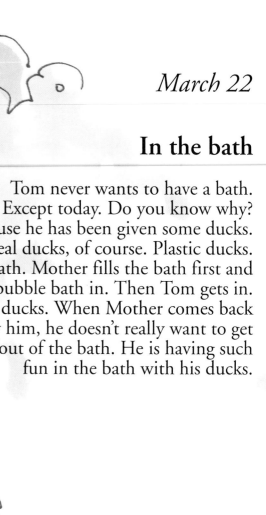

In the bath

Tom never wants to have a bath.
Except today. Do you know why?
Because he has been given some ducks.
Not real ducks, of course. Plastic ducks.
For his bath. Mother fills the bath first and
puts some bubble bath in. Then Tom gets in.
With his ducks. When Mother comes back
to dry him, he doesn't really want to get
out of the bath. He is having such
fun in the bath with his ducks.

March 23

The sleepy duckling

Can you see that duckling?
His name is Tired Jim.
He is a bit unusual,
He likes to sleep, does Jim.

On the bus or train,
At school or on the stair,
This yawning little duckling
Can sleep most anywhere!

March 24

A small duckling

Look, there is Miriam Duckling. She is still very small. She is wearing a diaper, just like a baby. Mother has already taught Miriam how to quack, so when she is hungry, she quacks as loudly as she can. But she's very quiet at the moment. Miriam is tired. She's almost asleep in the warm sunshine. That's fine, though, because Mother Duck is watching over her.

March 25

A worm with feet?

Martin and Rick Duckling are playing by the pond. "Hey, look at this," says Martin. "Something is crawling on this leaf. What do you think it is? It looks a bit like a worm with legs." "That's not a worm," says Rick, "that's a caterpillar." "A caterpillar?" says Martin with surprise. "I've never heard of one of those. I know, I'll go and get a jam jar. We can put the caterpillar in it. Then we'll be able to look at it properly." So that's what they do.

March 26

What is the caterpillar doing?

"Look," says Martin Duckling to Rick his duckling friend.
"We put the caterpillar in the jam jar." Martin holds the jam jar
up for Rick to see. "It's not moving anymore. I wonder why?"
"I know why," says Rick. "The caterpillar is turning into a butterfly."
"A butterfly?" says Martin in amazement.
"Yes," says Rick. "First the caterpillar eats lots and lots, then,
when he's full, he goes to sleep in his cocoon."
"What does that funny word mean?" asks Martin.
"A cocoon is a sort of house that the caterpillar makes for itself to go to sleep in.
When it has slept for long enough, it comes out of the cocoon. But then
it isn't a caterpillar anymore; it is a butterfly," explains Rick.
"Gosh, that sounds a bit complicated," says Martin. "I don't believe a word of it."

A butterfly

Martin and Rick Duckling have their noses
squashed against the side of a jam jar. Inside the jam
jar is a caterpillar in its cocoon. Martin and Rick are
waiting for the caterpillar to turn into a butterfly.
"I can see something moving," says Martin.
The cocoon is moving very gently. Little legs appear,
then wings. The wings are still stuck together. After
the butterfly has been out of the cocoon for a little
while, the wings dry and separate.
"Look at the beautiful colors," says Rick.
"Yes," says Martin, "and you were absolutely right.
The caterpillar did turn into a butterfly after all."
Then they open the lid of the jam jar and
let the butterfly fly away.

March 28

A lovely train

Look, here comes Tom Duckling.
What has he got there? It is a train, a toy
train on a string. The engine is at the front.
There are four carriages. Tom is pulling his train
around the room. First around the chairs and
then around the sofa. And sometimes under the table.
I'd love to have a train like Tom's, wouldn't you?

A big duck

There once was a duckling
Who was very small.
And oh! How he wanted
To be very tall!

So he ate and he ate,
Twenty times every day.
Now he's twenty times bigger,
In every way.

He eats and he eats.
How I wish he would stop.
If he eats any more
I'm sure he'll go pop!

March 30

A musical duckling

Maria has a little brother. He is a sweet little baby with tiny hands and fingers. Sometimes he cries. A duck hangs from a string above his cradle. When Mother or Father pulls the string, the duck plays a lullaby. When Maria's baby brother hears the lullaby, he stops crying and goes back to sleep. Isn't that nice?

March 31

New friends

Richard has a real duck. Her name is Frances. Richard
and Frances are always together. If Richard goes for a walk
outside, Frances follows him. When Richard goes to bed,
Frances sleeps in a box by his bed. But one day Frances has
disappeared. Richard can't find her anywhere. He looks
everywhere, all over the house and outside too, but he can't
find her. Where could she be? Richard is very sad. He sits
down on the grass and cries. But look! Who's that over there?
It's Frances. But what's that behind her? Six baby ducklings!
Richard is very happy because Frances has come back.
And she has brought him six new duckling friends.
How lovely!

April 1

Joke day

Mandy and Freddy Duckling are sitting by the pond. Suddenly Freddy jumps up.
"Look out," he shouts, "there's a frog on your head!"
Mandy jumps up with a start.
"Help," she cries, and puts her hands up to her head.
But there's no frog there. Freddy falls over laughing.
"Ha, ha, got you," he says, "April fool!"
Mandy doesn't think it's a bit funny. She was really frightened.
"Oh," she says, "very funny. But I don't think your mother
will find that tear in your pants very funny, either."
Freddy looks down at his pants. "A tear?" he asks. "Where? I can't see it."
Now it's Mandy's turn to laugh.
"There isn't a tear in your pants. April fool!"

April 2

Wet!

"Are you coming swimming?"
Tom Duckling asks Eric Duckling.
Eric thinks it's too cold, but agrees to give
it a try. They walk to the pond together.
Eric dips his toe gingerly into the water.
"Brr, it's cold!" he says. Tom goes to dip
his toe into the water, too. But he is
standing a bit too close to the edge of
the pond. He begins to wobble
and…splash! He topples into the water.
He climbs out again quickly.
"The water really is cold." He shivers.
"What did I tell you?" says Eric.
Then they both go home to warm
themselves up.

April 3

Making a wish

Robbie and Donny Duckling are lying in the grass.
"You know what," says Robbie, "if I could make a wish, I would wish that
I were a pilot. Then I could fly airplanes all the time. High in the sky."
"Yes," says Donny, "that's a good wish. But I would wish that I were very, very rich.
So rich that I could buy anything I want." Robbie and Donny lie back and
imagine how it would be if their wishes came true. Have you got a wish?

April 4

Little ducks

See the little ducklings
Swimming one and all.
Yellow, fluffy and
Very, very small,
Because in the spring
They pop out of their eggs.
Waddle, waddle, squeak,
   squeak,
On their tiny legs.

April 5

A nettle

Elly Duckling is walking along the side of the stream. She is picking flowers for her mother. She has already picked a lot. Then she sees another pretty flower. Elly puts out her wing to pick it, but brushes against another plant that stings her. Ow, she thinks, that hurts! Elly rushes home. Mother looks at Elly's wing. There are some lumps on it. "You stung yourself on a nettle," says Mother. "A nettle is a plant that can sting you if you brush against it." Mother rubs some cream on the lumps and gives Elly a kiss. Nettle stings don't hurt for very long so Elly was soon happy again.

A necklace for Violet

Violet is sitting on the ground next to
Sammy, her cuddly duckling.
Violet is making a necklace. A necklace of
pretty, colored beads. She threads the beads
one by one on a string. First a blue bead,
then a red one. Then a yellow one and a
green one. She keeps going until the string is
full. Then she ties a knot in the end and
the necklace is finished. Violet puts
the necklace around her neck.
Sammy thinks she looks beautiful.
Do you?

April 7

Robin is writing

Robin is sitting at the table. He is writing.
He learned to write at school. Robin can
already write his own name. And *tree* and *fish*.
And another word. Can you guess what it is?
It is the word *duck*. When Robin has finished
writing he does a drawing next to each word.
So he has drawn a tree, a fish,
and a duck. Isn't he clever!

April 8

Tag

Harry Duckling is playing outside with his friends Keith and Joshua.
They are playing tag. Harry is "it." He tries to catch Keith and Joshua.
Yes, he's caught Joshua.
"You're it!" shouts Harry loudly. So now Joshua has to tag the others.
He chases after Keith and manages to tag him. Now it's Keith's turn to
be "it." They keep playing until all that running makes them hungry.
Then they go home for something to eat.

April 9

The first time

There is Mother Duck.
Behind her are five baby ducklings.
They are going to the pond.
The ducklings are going for their very
first swim today. Mother Duck goes first.
All the ducklings follow her very
carefully except the last one. He's a bit
frightened. He stops at the edge of the
water. Here comes Mother. She pushes
him gently into the water with her beak.
He's not frightened anymore.
The ducklings swim neatly behind
their mother. Don't they look lovely?

April 10

Ghosts?

Freddy Duckling is in bed. He can't sleep. He tosses and turns.
Then he hears a strange noise. It sounds a bit like footsteps.
All of a sudden he hears: "Whooo, whooo!" Freddy is terrified
and hides under the covers. Could it be a ghost?
"Whooo, whooo!" it goes again. Freddy doesn't dare move.
Then he hears someone laughing. Quietly at first, then louder and
louder. He knows that laugh. It sounds very like Mandy's laugh.
Freddy jumps out of bed and opens his bedroom door.
Who do you think is crouching there? Mandy!
She really had him scared, didn't she?

April 11

The bald duck

There once was a duck,
Short and stout.
But one fine day
All his feathers fell out.

One fell out first,
Then the rest.
A very bald duck.
(He'd better wear a vest!)

The doctor gave him
Some medicine (yuck!)
To make the feathers grow.
And they did. (What luck!)

April 12

New glasses

Look, there is Joe Duckling.
He has just got new glasses. His old ones
were broken. Joe can't see very clearly without
glasses. He sees blurry trees and blurry grass,
and if he's not very careful he bumps into
things. This is why he has a new pair of glasses.
So that he can see everything properly.

April 13

Painting eggs

Thomas and Otto are sitting at the kitchen table. Mother has boiled some eggs for them. But they're not going to eat them. No, they're going to paint them. Thomas picks up his brush and dips it in some paint. He paints a duck on one of the eggs. "It looks really good, doesn't it?" he says. Otto looks at Thomas's egg. "You are clever," he says. "I'm trying to paint a duck, too, but I can't get it right." Thomas and Otto keep painting. They paint lots more eggs – stripy ones, spotty ones – all sorts. But the egg with the duck on it is the best.

April 14

I am a duckling

I am a duckling
Inside this egg.
When I get out
I will stretch a leg.

I am a duckling,
Clever little me.
I'll break this shell
And I'll shout:"Whee hee!"

Going shopping

Ginny Duckling is going shopping. She is carrying a big bag.
There is a purse with money in the bag. Mother has also given her a shopping list.
Ginny can't read yet, but that doesn't matter. She just gives the list to the man
in the shop. He puts everything in the bag. Ginny pays him with money
from the purse. "Good-bye, Mr. Shop Assistant," says Ginny.
"Good-bye, Ginny," he replies. "See you next time!"

April 16

A nest in the grass

"Look," says Tim to his friend
Derek. Tim is pointing to
the grass by the pond.
"What do you think that is?" he asks.
"It's a nest," says Derek, "a nest
with eggs – duck eggs, I think."
There are four eggs in the nest.
A duck waddles up.
It sits down on the eggs.
That way they stay nice and warm.
"In a few days," says Derek,
"baby ducklings will hatch
out of the eggs."
"Really?" asks Tim.
"I can hardly wait!"

April 17

The purple duckling

I know a duckling,
Odd as can be.
Not like the others,
No, not he!

Do you know why?
His feathers aren't brown.
This duckling is purple
From his toes to his crown.

April 18

Hair washing

"Karl, are you coming?" calls Karl's mother. She is in the bathroom, because it is time for Karl to have a shower. Here comes Karl. He is carrying Doris, his cuddly duckling. Karl doesn't mind having a shower. He does mind having his hair washed. And today is hair-washing day. "I know what we'll do," says Mother. "I'll wash your hair and you can wash Doris's hair." Karl thinks this is a good idea. He puts some shampoo on Doris's head and rubs it in well. Then he rinses it off under the shower. There, Doris has lovely clean hair again. While he was busy with Doris, Mother washed Karl's hair and he didn't even notice!

April 19

The eggs hatch

Tim and Derek are sitting together on the grass next to the pond. They are looking at the duck's nest. There are four eggs in the nest. "Look," says Tim, "one of the eggs is moving." First a tiny beak appears, then a head and a tiny body with wings and legs. The other eggs begin to move, too. Very soon there are four baby ducklings in the nest. Don't they look lovely?

April 20

Feeding the birds

"I think the baby ducks are hungry," says Tim to his friend Derek. "Of course they're hungry," says Derek. Tim and Derek are looking at the little ducklings opening their beaks wide. "What do ducklings eat?" asks Tim. "Just watch," replies Derek. Here comes Mother Duck. She sees Tim and Derek and is a bit frightened. "Come on," says Derek, "we'd better go away and leave the mother duck to look after her babies. She's frightened of us." When the ducklings are big enough to swim, Tim and Derek go back to look at them again.

April 21

Party

Today there is a big party in Hans's village. All the streets are decorated with flags, but the decorated floats are the best. All the children are allowed to sit on the floats as they drive around the streets, but they have to be dressed up. Frank, Hans's friend, is dressed as a monkey. Ellen is a cat, and Hans, of course, is wearing a duck costume. He has lovely feathers and a big, red beak.

When Hans is on the float he begins to quack very loudly so that all the people look at him. He waves to them with his duck's wing. The float drives on through the village and everyone waves. It is an excellent party.

April 22

Afraid of the dark

When Erica is in bed at night and all
the lights are out, she is sometimes
afraid. Not always, just now and then.
But she has discovered what to do so
that she isn't afraid anymore. She creeps
down under the covers with Johnny, her
cuddly duckling. She cuddles him very
tight. Then she makes up a nice story to
tell him. If she does this, she isn't
afraid anymore. Well done, Erica.

April 23

The duckling from Kent

There once was a duckling
Who lived in Kent.
He had a small problem,
His beak was all bent.

So each time he ate,
Or drank, or smiled,
He had to turn
His head to one side.

81

Annette can walk

Today is Annette's birthday.
Her first birthday. The whole day is
one long party. Grandma and Grandpa
are here and have brought Annette a
big present. It is a big teddy bear,
almost as big as Annette herself and
lovely and soft. Annette has a birthday
cake and lemonade, and is allowed to
blow out the one candle on the cake.
Then Aunt Mary arrives. She has also
brought a present for the birthday girl.
"Come on, walk over to me,"
she says to Annette. Annette manages
to walk the few steps to Aunt Mary,
but she has only just learned how to
do it and is still a bit wobbly.
"Look what I've brought you,"
says Aunt Mary. She unwraps
a beautiful wooden duck with bells
on it. A string is tied onto its beak
so that Annette can pull it along
behind her on its little wheels.
The bells jingle as it rides along.
The duck is definitely
Annette's favorite present.

82

April 25

In a row

Look at us swimming
All in a row.
Mother at the front,
We're all in tow.

Look at us swimming,
Waggling our feet.
We're swimming quickly.
Soon we will eat.

Peter will feed us
Bread and some crumbs.
We will eat lots and lots,
Filling our tums.

April 26

Cilla can't sleep

Cilla Duckling is lying in bed. She can't get to sleep. Do you
know why? Because it is her birthday tomorrow. She can't stop
thinking about the presents she might get. Perhaps a book, or a
doll, or some marbles or perhaps a jigsaw puzzle. Or even…
Cilla falls asleep. Perhaps she is dreaming about all the presents
she would like to get tomorrow.

April 27

A cake with candles

Cilla Duckling wakes up very early in the morning. Today is her birthday. She could hardly get to sleep last night for thinking about it. When she comes downstairs she sees a lovely big cake on the table. A cake with four candles, because Cilla is four years old today. At dessert time, Mother lights the candles and Cilla may blow them out. She takes a deep breath and blows them all out in one breath. Then everybody gets a big piece of the delicious cake.

April 28

Storm

The ducks are all gathered together down by the pond. It is raining, but that doesn't bother ducks. They don't mind a bit of water. But what is that? There is a flash in the sky and then a loud bang. The little ducks are afraid, but the big ducks begin to laugh. "Don't be frightened, little ones," they say, "it's only a storm. Look at the sky, then you'll see how beautiful the flashes of lightning are!" The little ducks look up at the lightning flashes with amazement. Yes, they are beautiful, but they're still just a little bit frightened.

April 29

Listen here

Listen here,
Can you see?
I wear a hat!
Smart old me.

Won't you come,
Oh, please do!
There'll be cake,
Lemonade, too!

April 30

The queen's birthday

Today is the queen's birthday. Everyone is celebrating. The streets are decorated and there are lots of flags flying. It looks very festive. The flag is flying outside Bert's house, too. He helped his father put it up. Do you know what else Bert has done? He has decorated Waddle, his cuddly duck. Waddle is now wearing a lovely orange bow. A big one. Bert is very proud that Waddle looks so smart. I think Waddle is prouder still.

May 1

A strange egg

Josie is in the garden. What's that lying on the ground? It's an egg.
But it's not a hen's egg. It is much bigger and a different color.
Josie picks it up carefully and takes it into the house.
"Mother, come and look," she calls out. "I've found an egg."
"Hey, that's a duck's egg," says Mother. "We'll put it in a box with a blanket.
Then it will stay nice and warm." And that's just what they do.

May 2

The egg hatches

Josie is looking at the egg. It is lying in a box with a blanket.
Josie found the egg in the garden. It is a duck's egg.
But what's happening? The egg is beginning to move.
"Mother, come quickly," calls out Josie, "the egg is moving."
Mother comes to look. A crack appears in the egg.
Then a little hole. The hole gets bigger and bigger until a
tiny beak pops out. Followed by the rest of a tiny duckling.
"Peep, peep," it says. Josie gives the duckling some food.
Then the baby duckling goes to sleep on the blanket
in its box. Night night, Duckling, sleep tight.

A duck on wheels

Bert is in the shed with Father. Do you know what they are doing? They are making a duck. Not a real duck, of course, but a wooden duck. First Father sawed a duck out of a piece of wood. Now Bert's job is to sandpaper the duck until it is nice and smooth. Father is now making some wheels so that the duck will be able to roll along. When Bert has finished sandpapering, Father puts the wheels on. There, that's finished. Now it's time to paint the duck. Father gets some paint and two brushes. Bert and Father paint the duck in lovely bright colors. They paint the body red and the wings purple. Bert gives it a lovely orange beak, and black eyes. Last of all they paint the wheels blue. Then Father attaches a piece of rope to the beak and the duck is completely finished. Isn't the duck beautiful? Bert and Father are very proud of their handiwork.

May 4

Mother is gone

In among the rushes
Is a duckling sad and small.
He has lost his mother.
He can't find her, not at all.

He was swimming quietly
Behind his mother dear.
Then she swam off quickly
And left him in the rear.

He's sitting in a corner,
Everything looks so black.
But look, yes, wait a minute,
Who do I see coming back?

May 5

Hanging out the washing

Elsie is in the garden with her mother. They are hanging out the washing. Elsie has a little brother. A little brother who still wears diapers, the old-fashioned sort of diapers that need washing. When all the diapers have been washed, they need to be hung out to dry. Elsie is allowed to help. She passes the clothespins to Mother. Do you know who else is helping? Elsie's cuddly duck. He's guarding the washing line.

May 6

A grumpy day

Harland Duckling is sitting at the edge of the pond. He has a very cross face.
Harland doesn't feel like doing anything today. His friend Otto comes up to him.
"Hello, Harland, are you coming to play ball?" he asks. "No," says Harland grumpily.
"Why not?" asks Otto. "It would be fun." "I don't want to play," says Harland.
"I don't feel like playing. I'm in a bad mood today."
"Fine," says Otto, "I'll play by myself then." Otto goes away. He jumps into the
water with the ball. He is quickly joined by lots of other ducklings.
Harland looks at Otto and the other ducklings. They're enjoying themselves.
He begins to feel a bit left out. He goes over to them. "May I still play with you?"
he asks. "Of course," replies Otto. They all play together happily, and Harland
forgets all about being grumpy today.

May 7

Lots of cuddly toys

Annemarie is in her room. She is drinking tea. But not by herself. She is having a tea party with all her cuddly toys. She has lots of them. A monkey, a bear, an elephant and a rabbit. But her favorite is a duck.
She loves the other cuddly animals, but she loves Duck a little bit more.
They're all sitting in a circle, drinking tea.
Isn't that nice?

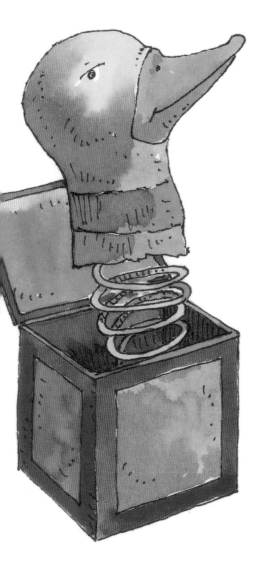

May 8

The duck-in-the-box

"Mother," calls Sammy very loudly, "where are you?"
"I'm in the kitchen," she replies. Sammy goes to the kitchen. He has a box in his hand.
"Look," says Sammy, and shows the box to Mother.
"What a nice box," says Mother. "Is there anything inside it?" "Just watch," says Sammy, and presses a button. The box opens and a duck jumps out.
A duck on a spring. Mother gets a fright. She hadn't expected that. "Gosh, you made me jump," she says.
Sammy just laughs. He really had Mother fooled.

Still in the egg

Timmy Duckling wakes up. "Where am I?" he wonders. He looks around.
Everywhere is dark, very dark. It is as if he is in a tiny, dark house. A house with
around walls. Timmy pushes his beak against the wall. The wall moves and cracks.
Light comes in through the crack. He pokes his head out through the crack.
Do you know what he can see? Lots more eggs with cracks in them. Out of each
egg comes a duckling. These are Timmy's brothers and sisters. Mother Duck is
there too. She looks very happy. She has four new baby ducklings.

May 10

Knock, knock

Knock, knock, knock,
Now listen to me.
Out of this egg
I'll break, you see!

Knock, knock, knock,
I'm nearly through,
And out I creep
As new as new!

May 11

A vain duckling

Kurt Duckling thinks he is very handsome. He is a vain duckling.
He's almost always looking in the mirror, at least a hundred times a day.
He looks to check that his feathers are smooth, or to see if his tail is nice and shiny, or sometimes to polish his beak. Kurt is constantly preening himself.
There are lots of mirrors in Kurt's house. One in every room, so that he can always look at himself. I'd much prefer to go outside to play. Wouldn't you?

May 12

Jonathan finds something

Jonathan is down by the stream. He is looking for
tadpoles. Suddenly he hears a squeak.
What could it be? Jonathan looks around.
He spies a tiny duckling in the rushes.
It is all alone. Very carefully, Jonathan picks
the duckling up. It is a bit frightened at first.
Then Jonathan puts it under his nice, warm sweater.
When he gets home, he gives it some bread and water,
then puts it in a box. The duckling goes to sleep.
He's not alone or afraid anymore.

May 13

Back to the stream

Jonathan has a duckling at home in a box. He found it by the stream.
It was all alone and frightened. Jonathan has taken good care of the little duckling.
It has had some food and drink and a good sleep. Jonathan picks up the duckling
very carefully. He is going to take it back to the stream.
Jonathan puts the duckling back in the water. And look, here comes Mother Duck.
She had been rather worried. But now she has her duckling back again.
He swims straight up to his mother and joins his brother and sister ducklings.
Jonathan waves good-bye to them. Good-bye!

May 14

Clouds

Mark and Peter Duckling are lying in
the grass. They are looking at the
clouds in the sky. "Look at that one,"
says Mark. "It looks just like an elephant."
"What about that one," says Peter,
"it looks like a clown. No, it doesn't
anymore. The wind is blowing it.
It looks like a…" "…duck!" says Mark.
"Yes," says Peter, "like a duck."
"This is fun, isn't it?" says Peter.
"Much more fun than school. I'd like
to lie here watching clouds all the time.
Except when it's raining of course,
because we'd get wet."

May 15

Sneaking candy

Edward Duckling is in the kitchen. He would really like some candy.
The candy jar is on the cupboard. Nobody would notice, would they,
if he just took one? He climbs up on a chair. He opens the jar and takes out
a piece of candy. Quickly he pops it in his beak and puts the lid back on the
jar. He gets down from the chair. Mother comes into the kitchen.
"What are you doing?" she asks. Edward hides the candy under his tongue.
"Oh, nothing," he answers. "Are you sure?" asks Mother. Edward nods,
but his cheeks turn a little red. Perhaps he should have asked first.

The duck in the tree

There once was a duckling
From Clacton-on-Sea.
And guess what? That duckling
Loved climbing a tree.

The others called out:
"Come down here and swim?"
The duckling stayed put.
Swimming wasn't for him.

"Oh no," said the duckling,
"It's here I must be.
It's nice being different,
High up in a tree!"

May 17

Jessie gets a postcard

"Jessie, will you see if there's any mail today?" calls Mother from the kitchen.
Jessie goes to look. She hopes there will be a letter for her. There is a newspaper
on the doormat. A letter for Father and a postcard are lying there, too. The card
has a picture of a duck on it. Who could the card be for? Jessie turns it over.
"To Jessie, from Grandpa and Grandma," it says.
Isn't that nice? Jessie takes the mail to Mother, but she takes the duck postcard
to her bedroom. She hangs it up above her bed. It does look nice.
Jessie is very happy.

May 18

Chicken pox

Harriet is in bed. She is ill.
She has chicken pox.
She has red lumps everywhere: on her
arms, her legs, her tummy, and on her
back. The doctor has been to visit.
He said that Harriet must stay in bed
for a few days. Then the chicken pox
will go away all by itself. Mother still
feels a bit sorry for Harriet. So she has
bought her a lovely cuddly duckling.
Harriet cuddles her new duckling tight.
She feels a bit better already.

May 19

Counting on your fingers

Vincent and Susan are sitting on the sofa.
Vincent's cuddly duckling is sitting next to them.
Vincent and Susan are doing something very
difficult. They are counting. Not on paper, on
their fingers. "Here are two fingers," says Vincent.
"If I add two more fingers, that will make four."
Duck doesn't understand. "I understand," says
Susan, "and if I add one more finger to your four
fingers, that will make five. Look, five fingers!"
She holds up her hand. Vincent and Duck look at
Susan's hand. They count the fingers together.
The thumb is one, forefinger is two, middle
finger is three, ring finger is four, and little
finger is five. Exactly right! Aren't they clever?

The rainbow

It is raining. Big, fat raindrops are falling on the ground. Mandy and Freddy Duckling are looking at the rain. "Yuck," says Freddy, "I hate the rain. We can't play outside." He makes a face. Mandy isn't very happy, either. But then the sun appears through the clouds. "Oh, look," says Mandy, "look at all those colors in the sky. What do you think it is?" "That is a rainbow," says Freddy. "When the sun shines on the rain it makes an arch of lovely colors called a rainbow. Isn't it pretty?" Mandy and Freddy watch the rainbow until it disappears.

May 21

Together in the shopping cart

Sandra is out shopping with her mother. Sammy, Sandra's toy duck, has come too. Do you know what they like best about going shopping? They like sitting in the shopping cart together. Mother pushes the cart and puts the shopping in it. Sandra and Sammy look around at all the things in the store. What a lot there are!
And they don't get a bit tired, because they don't have to walk. Aren't they lucky!

May 22

The duck from Dundee

There once was a duckling
Who lived in Dundee.
Guess what, that duckling
Just wanted to wee.

Wherever he was,
He cried out: "Oh no!
The bathroom is where
I really must go!"

His mother then thought
That to make him happy
She should give him
  a diaper,
Though some call it
  a nappy.

May 23

A duck on a string

Simon is walking along the side of the stream. He has brought his duck with him.
It isn't a real duck but a wooden one. On a string. Simon lets his duck float along the
stream. When he pulls the string the duck swims forward. It looks just as if the duck
is really swimming. A couple of real ducks look at the wooden duck. They make a face.
They can't understand where the new duck has come from. But we know, don't we?

May 24

To the circus

Thomas is going to the circus with his parents. He's allowed to take his toy duck Kooky with him. There is a long line in front of the circus tent. Father goes to buy the tickets and then they go inside. They find seats close to the ring. Soon the ringmaster appears. He is wearing a very smart black suit. He is the boss of the circus. Then come the elephants. Gosh, aren't they big and strong, and aren't they clever doing all those tricks? After the elephants come the lions and tigers. Thomas is afraid of the wild animals, so he cuddles his duck extra tight. Kooky closes his eyes, because he thinks the lions and tigers look rather like big cats. Then it's the acrobats in the ring. They climb on top of each other and do all sorts of dangerous balancing tricks without falling. There's a clown too. He is so funny that Thomas gets a tummy ache from laughing so much. At last, the show is over. Everyone goes home. Thomas and Kooky don't really want to go home. They had such a lovely time at the circus that they'd like to go every day!

Green paint

Mandy and Freddy Duckling are helping Freddy's father with some painting. The front door needs a new coat of paint. Mandy and Freddy have each been given a can of paint and a brush. They are each allowed to paint half the door. Freddy is doing the right-hand side and Mandy the left. Freddy carefully dips his brush in the pot of green paint. He brushes the paint on the door.
"No, don't do that," says Mandy, "that's my half of the door."
"It's not," says Freddy. "Yes, it is," says Mandy. They begin to argue, and green paint gets spattered everywhere. Then along comes Freddy's father. "What are you two doing?" he asks. Freddy and Mandy stop arguing and look at each other. They're both covered in green paint. There's green paint everywhere, except on the door. They start to laugh. They look so funny with all that green paint on them. Luckily Father thinks it's funny too.

May 26

An old cuddly duck

Jerry is in the living room. He is looking at a photograph on the cupboard.
It is a picture of a small boy and girl wearing funny clothes. They look rather strange.
The boy is holding something in his hand. It looks like a duck.
"Father," says Jerry, "who are these children in the photograph?"
"That's me," says Father, "and that's Aunt Lucy. I was five then, as you are now."
"But you look so funny," says Jerry. "You're wearing such strange clothes."
"I know," says Father, "but that was quite normal then. Can you see what I was
holding? It was my cuddly duck, Timmy."
"Have you still got him?" asks Jerry.
"Perhaps," says Father, and goes to look in the attic. He comes back a bit later with
the duck in his hands. "I'm too big for a toy duck these days, so you can have him,"
he says to Jerry. He gives the duck to Jerry, and then he fetches his camera. He has
decided that it would be nice to take a picture of Jerry with Timmy the duck.

May 27

The duck with the trumpet

A duckling with a trumpet
Had a room in a house.
He trumpeted all day long
And scared a little mouse!

He played it on the roof,
He played it in the yard.
The noise he made was very loud,
He blew so very hard.

The other ducklings in the house
Put cotton in their ears.
They feared he might be playing
For years and years and years!

May 28

Swimming

Little ducklings
Swimming in the water.
Fol-de-rol-de-ray.

Little ducklings
Swimming in the water.
All the day!

Puppies

Something special has happened today. Bert's dog has had puppies. Three puppies. They are lying in a box with their mother. They are still tiny and can't walk yet. Their eyes are still closed. Bert is sitting next to the box looking at the puppies with his toy duck Flappy. "Aren't they tiny and sweet?" says Bert to Flappy. "They can hardly do anything. All they can do is drink their mother's milk and crawl a bit." Bert and Flappy love looking at the puppies. They think they're so nice.

May 30

In the park

Lisa is in the park with Grandma. They are sitting on a bench and watching the ducks on the pond. There are lots of ducks. Some are brown and some are white. Lisa likes watching the ducks. So does Grandma. So they go to the park often and take some stale bread with them. When they feed it to them, the ducks come right up close to Lisa. The boldest one even takes the bread from Lisa's hand!

May 31

Mowing the lawn

Barry is outside with his father.
Do you know what they are doing?
They are mowing the lawn. Father
is mowing and Barry is raking the
cut grass together into a big pile.
Barry's toy duck is sitting on a chair.
He is watching to see that they do
everything right. When Barry has
raked together a big pile of grass, he
puts it into the wheelbarrow. It looks
nice and tidy. But raking is thirsty
work. Mother comes outside,
bringing the workers big glasses of
lemonade. Just what Barry needed!
Mmm, delicious. But there's no
lemonade for Duck because he's
fallen asleep at his post.
Well, the sun was so lovely and
warm. Sleep well, Duck.

June 1

Getting married

Mandy and Freddy Duckling are playing up in the attic. They are dressing up.
Mandy has put on a pretty pink dress and a silly hat. Freddy is wearing a smart suit
with a black top hat. They are getting married. Not really, just pretend.
"Oh dear, these are very wobbly," says Mandy. She is tottering around
in a pair of bright pink, high-heeled shoes that are far too big for her.
Freddy's shoes are too big for him too, but they haven't got high heels.
"Come on, husband," says Mandy, "let's go and have a cup of tea."
"Good idea, wife," says Freddy, and they walk off together very grandly.

June 2

The duck who
wanted to marry

"Who will marry me?"
Said the duck.
No one answered.
No such luck.

He traveled the world.
Far and near.
No one would have him.
Dear, oh dear.

Lily gets a bicycle

Today is Lily's birthday. She has been given
a very big present. A beautiful red bicycle.
It has two big wheels and two small wheels.
The small wheels are next to the big wheels,
one on each side. They keep Lily from falling
over. But there's more. The bicycle has a basket
attached to the handlebars. Lily puts
her toy duck in it. They have
great fun biking together.

June 4

A sore knee

John is roller skating on the pavement. He's not
allowed on the road, because there are far too
many cars. But he is allowed on the pavement.
John is very good at roller skating. He's going very
fast. Oh dear, there's a stone sticking up, right in
John's path. He doesn't notice it and…crash!
John falls and grazes his knee. Ow, that hurts.
His knee is bleeding a bit, so he goes home as
quickly as he can. Mother puts a Band-Aid on his
sore knee. A Band-Aid with a picture of a duck on
it. It is much nicer than an ordinary Band-Aid.
Mother gives the sore knee a kiss. I think John's
knee will be better very soon, don't you?

June 5

Dog poo

Mandy and Freddy Duckling are walking along the pavement together. They are on their way home from school.
"Wasn't that a lovely story the teacher told us?" says Mandy, "except the end was a bit sad."
"Yes," agrees Freddy, "and…" but he doesn't finish his sentence because Mandy begins to scream. "Look out, dog poo!" she shouts, but it is too late. Freddy has stepped right in it. He makes a face. "Yuck, that really smells horrible," says Freddy. Mandy has a little laugh. "Well, I did try to warn you," she says with a grin, "but it was too late." Freddy wipes the poo off on the curb, then runs home to get the rest off his shoe. He'll certainly look where he's going next time!

June 6

A large basket of fruit

Francis Duckling's teacher is ill. There is another teacher at school in her place. This teacher is nice, but not as nice as Francis's real teacher. All the ducklings in Francis's class have made a surprise present for their sick teacher. It is a large basket of fruit. Each duckling brought some fruit to school – an apple, an orange, a tangerine, or a banana. And lots more, too, so that the basket is full to the brim. This afternoon two of the ducklings are going to take the basket of fruit to their teacher. That will make her feel much better, don't you think?

June 7

A clever idea

Tim and Tom Duckling are sitting by the pond. They are a bit bored.
"I know," says Tom, "let's play hide-and-seek."
"Good idea," says Tim. "I'll hide first and you can come and look for me."
"Okay," says Tom, and closes his eyes. He counts to ten, then opens his eyes again.
Where could Tim be? He can't see him anywhere. Not behind a tree or a bush.
Not in among the reeds either. Hold on a minute, though, there's a reed sticking
out of the water. Reeds don't normally wobble like that, do they? Then Tom
realizes where Tim is. He is underwater, breathing air through a reed.
Wasn't that a clever place to hide?

The duck from Delft

I have heard tell
Of a duck from Delft
Who went to sea
All by himself.

A big wave came,
Ten leagues high.
No more duck.
Farewell, good-bye.

June 9

Delicious cakes

Edward Duckling is sitting on the sofa. His mother has visitors and the room is full of grown-up ducks. Edward is not enjoying himself. He goes to the kitchen. There is a plate of delicious cakes on the kitchen table. It gives Edward an idea. If he were to take just one cake, do you think the big ducks would notice? He takes one. Nobody notices him. Then he takes another, and another. Edward keeps eating cakes until they are nearly all gone. And nobody has noticed. Edward goes back to the living room and sits down contentedly on the sofa. Nobody can explain why he looks so happy. But we know, don't we?

Handsome Karl

Handsome Karl, the good-looking duckling, was walking proudly along the bank of the stream. His feathers gleamed and he was very proud of himself. He was, as usual, more concerned about how he looked than where he was going. One minute he was walking along, the next he was in the water. He had slipped. Normally this wouldn't matter, because Karl is a good swimmer, but the water in the stream was very dirty. And muddy.
Lots of ducklings rushed up to help Karl. They had to watch out that they didn't fall in, too, as they tried to help him out with sticks and pieces of wood. Eventually, after lots of attempts, they managed to get poor Karl onto the side. He was so dirty! His feathers were all stuck together with mud.
You could hardly call him Handsome Karl anymore.
Grubby Karl would be much better.

June 11

A rabbit in danger

Bea and Iris Duckling are down by the pond in the
wood. Suddenly they hear someone shouting.
"Help! Help!" they hear. Bea and Iris look at
each other. "Who do you think it is?" asks Iris.
"I don't know," says Bea, "let's go and look."
"Help! Help!" goes the voice again. Bea and Iris look
around. "Look over there! A rabbit!" says Bea.
They rush over to it.
"What's the matter?" asks Bea.
"I was playing," says the rabbit, "and all of a sudden
I got my foot stuck in this hole. I can't get it out."
"Don't worry," says Iris, "we'll help you."
Bea and Iris make the hole bigger, so that the
little rabbit can pull his foot out.
"Hurray," says the rabbit, "I'm free again. Thank you
very much indeed." He hops off into the wood.
"Good-bye, little rabbit," call Bea and Iris,
"and do be careful!"

113

A fat tummy

Sandra's mother has a very fat tummy. Do you know why? Because there is a baby inside. Mother is sitting on the sofa. Sandra is sitting next to her with her duck. "Can you hear the baby?" asks Sandra. "Try and see," says Mother. Sandra puts her ear on Mother's tummy. "Hey, he's kicking my cheek!" she says. Sandra puts her cuddly duck on Mother's tummy so he can feel the baby, too. He rocks back and forth. Poor Duck isn't sure what's happening. The baby must be very good at kicking. Mother laughs. Luckily the kicking doesn't hurt. It won't be very long now before the baby is born.

June 13

Mother has a baby

Sandra's mother is in bed. She isn't ill, but she has just had a baby. A little boy. Sandra now has a little brother. She is very proud of him. She stands next to the cradle with her duck. "Isn't he sweet?" Sandra says to Duck, "and he's so tiny. Look at his tiny hands and tiny fingers." Sandra can hardly believe that she once had tiny hands and fingers just like that. But she did. And so did you.

June 14

The duck from Liverpool

There was a duck from Liverpool,
I think you'll know him well.
Now listen to this little tale
That I am going to tell.

He'd seven pairs of pants,
And seven sweaters too.
He'd seven pairs of funny shoes.
And caps? He'd quite a few.

The funniest thing of all was,
He wore them all together.
All on top and underneath,
No matter what the weather.

June 15

An annoying mosquito

Derek Duckling is so tired that he is nearly asleep. Suddenly there is a noise. "Bzzz, bzzz," goes the noise. What could it be? Derek turns on the light and looks around. "Bzzz, bzzz," it goes again. Then silence. Derek notices a black insect on the wall. A mosquito. He won't be able to sleep as long as the mosquito is in his room. He gets out of bed. He creeps very quietly over to the mosquito, puts out his wing and…yes, got it! He opens the window and lets it fly away. Now he can go to sleep. Good night, Derek, sleep tight!

A pair of mucky ducklings

Mandy and Freddy Duckling are sitting at the kitchen table.
They have just finished supper and are having some custard for dessert.
"Eek!" screams Mandy suddenly.
"What's the matter?" asks Freddy.
"Yuck, there's a fly in your custard." Mandy points at Freddy's bowl.
"A fly?" says Freddy. "Where? I can't see one." He bends down to look at his custard
more closely. Mandy gives his head a push, right into the custard. She thinks it's
very funny. "Ha, ha," she laughs, "did you find the fly in your custard?"
Freddy doesn't think it's at all funny.
"Funny? I don't think so," he says, "in fact, just as funny as that hair in your custard."
"A hair in my custard?" says Mandy, and looks down at her bowl.
And yes, Freddy does the same to her. Mandy's face is covered in custard.
Now Freddy thinks that is very funny. "Did you find the hair?" he says.
Mother comes into the kitchen. "What have you two been doing?" she asks.
"You pair of dirty ducklings, go and wash your faces this minute!"

June 17

The camera

Danny Duckling has a camera.
Not a real camera, but the kind you
put water in. "Mother," says Danny,
"may I take a picture of you?"
"Of course," says Mother.
"Right," says Danny, "stand here
and smile." Danny presses the
button and a jet of water shoots
out of the camera.
"I'm all wet!" says Mother.
"Got you!" says Danny,
and runs away quickly.

June 18

On the boat

Gerard Duckling's father has a boat. It is a big boat with a mast and sails.
Gerard quite often goes sailing on the boat with his father. He's allowed to help
steer the boat, which is quite difficult. Do you know what Gerard likes doing best?
He likes sitting at the back of the boat dangling his feet in the water.
It tickles and makes his feet nice and cool.

Tying shoelaces

Kevin has new shoes. Brightly colored shoes with laces. Mother shows him how to tie the laces. First you make a loop with one lace. Then you wind the other lace around it. Last you pull the first one through the second one. And that's it! It looks very easy when Mother does it. But Kevin will have to practice. His fingers get all tangled up. Kevin's toy duck is sitting watching. He thinks it's quite funny. Kevin is so clumsy. But then he does it right. His laces are tied. That really is very clever of Kevin. He looks down at his new shoes very proudly. Duck is proud of him too.

June 20

To the moon

There once was a duck
Who ate with a spoon.
And that duck said:
"I am off to the moon!"

So he built a great rocket,
It was seven leagues high.
And in that big rocket
He flew up to the sky.

When you look at the moon
On a very dark night,
You may just see the duck –
If he's left on the light!

June 21

Cake bobbing

It is Hilary Duckling's birthday
and she is giving a party.
She has invited ten of her friends.
Mother has thought up a good
game: cake bobbing.
Mother has tied pieces of string
to the washing line, and there is a
piece of cake on each one. All the
children must put their hands
behind their backs and try to eat
a piece of cake. Whoever finishes
their cake first has won.
Everyone is standing next to
the washing line. Mother counts
to three, then they may start.
One, two, three…all the
ducklings are doing their best.
And they all finish together!
What a delicious game!

June 22

A trip to the playground

Each time Eric Duckling visits his grandma and grandpa they go to the playground.
It isn't far away. At the playground there is a swing, a seesaw, and a junglegym.
Eric likes the swing best, especially when Grandpa pushes him, because then he goes
really high. So high that he can nearly see over the tops of the trees. On the way home,
Grandma buys him an ice cream. I wish I were Eric, don't you?

June 23

Watering the plants together

Jenny is in the garden. She has Duck next to her. Jenny is watering the plants and Duck is helping her. The watering can is quite heavy, but together they manage to lift it. They water all the flowers. Haven't Jenny and Duck done a good job?

June 24

A beautiful kite

Hans is playing in a field. He has brought his kite with him. It is a beautiful kite. It looks like a duck and has a long tail with lots of colored bows on it. Hans throws the duck kite up into the sky. There it goes. Hans had better hold on to the string or his lovely kite will fly away. It looks beautiful up there in the sky with its tail waving in the wind. It is a very special kite: you'd think there was a real duck with a long tail flying up there.

June 25

Gertie is lost!

Something dreadful has happened. Jasper went on the train to visit Grandma and took Gertie, his cuddly duck, with him. Then Jasper got off the train and left Gertie behind. Jasper is at the station. He is almost crying, because the train with Gertie on it has already left the station. What should he do? Here comes a man in a blue uniform. It is the ticket collector. "Why, young man," says the ticket collector, "whatever is the matter?" "Well," gasps Jasper, "I went to visit Grandma with my cuddly duck, Gertie, and now I've left Gertie on the train!" Big, fat tears roll down Jasper's cheeks. "Now, now," says the ticket collector, "just leave it to me. Come along with me, and I'll see what I can do." Together they walk to a little office where there are some other ticket collectors. "You sit down here," says the ticket collector, "and I'll go and see if I can find Gertie." Jasper has to wait a little while, but then the man comes back. Gertie is in his hands! Jasper is so relieved to have Gertie back again. "Thank you very much, Mr. Ticket Collector," says Jasper, and runs home holding Gertie very tightly.

The talkative duckling

There once was a duckling
Who talked all day.
He quacked during school,
And he quacked while at play.

His mother said: "Stop.
That's enough for this week.
I'll buy some tape
To wrap around your beak!"

June 27

A lovely bunch of flowers

Frank Duckling is in the garden.
He is picking flowers for his mother.
He already has a big handful. There are
yellow flowers, red flowers, pink ones
and white ones too. When Frank has
picked enough flowers he goes inside.
He gives them to his mother.
Mother is very pleased with
them and puts them in a vase.
They look lovely.

June 28

Jacob in two

Carolyn and Clara are arguing about Jacob, the cuddly duck.
"He's mine," says Carolyn and holds him tight.
"No, he's not, he's mine," says Clara, and grabs Jacob from Carolyn.
"Mine!" says Carolyn and pulls at Jacob's head. But Clara won't let him go.
They both pull hard and…Jacob tears in two. Right down the middle.
Carolyn and Clara are startled. They sit down on the ground each holding half
of Jacob. Here comes Mother. "What a lot of noise you two are making," she says,
"what on earth are you…" Then she notices Jacob. "Have you two been fighting
over Jacob?" she asks. Carolyn and Clara nod.
"Give him to me," says Mother, "and I'll fix him. Go and play something else,
but no more arguing." Carolyn and Clara are too shocked to argue anymore.
For today, at least.

A real doctor?

Mandy and Freddy Duckling are playing doctors. Mandy is the doctor and Freddy the patient. "What is the matter, sir?" asks Mandy. "Well," says Freddy, "my beak is bothering me."
"Let me take a look," says Mandy. "Ah yes, I see the problem. It doesn't look good. I'll have to bandage it." Mandy gets out a large roll of bandage. "Come over here," she says, "and we'll have that beak bandaged in no time."
Mandy winds the bandage around Freddy's beak, but she goes on and on, until you can't see any beak at all. "Mmmm, mmmmm," mumbles Freddy. He can't talk through all that bandage. "Now then, no grumbling," says Mandy. "This bandage has to stay on for a few days, then your beak won't hurt anymore."
Do you think she was telling the truth?

June 30

A mosquito?

Father Duck is snoozing on the sofa. Simon comes into the room. He has a feather in his hand. He tickles Father very gently under the beak with it. Father shakes his head and mumbles something, but doesn't wake up. Simon does it again. This time Father rubs his face and scratches his beak. He still doesn't wake up. Simon tries it a third time. Father wakes up. "What was that?" he says." My beak keeps itching." Simon holds the feather behind his back and says: "Oh, I think it was a mosquito." "A mosquito?" says Father with amazement. Simon nods. "Oh well, you may be right," says Father. He turns over and goes to sleep again. Simon's trick worked, didn't it?

July 1

Out for a walk

Irene Duckling is out for a walk. First she goes to the pond. There are lots of things to see there. Frogs and fish swim in the water and dragonflies fly around above it. Then Irene goes on a bit further to the field. There are cows and horses there. A bit further on there are sheep too. Irene is rather tired after all that walking. She sits down and leans against a tree. The sun is so lovely and warm. Irene falls asleep. Ssh, be very quiet, or else you might wake Irene up.

July 2

Wilhelmina Duckling

Naughty Wilhelmina Duckling
Went into the field alone,
Without asking, without thinking.
Too small to be on her own!

Off she waddled through the grass,
Pretty flowers, like a dream,
Quite forgetting night was falling.
"I must go back to the stream!"

All alone and far from water,
Wilhelmina was afraid.
Then she heard somebody quacking.
Father Duck come to her aid!

Wilhelmina was so happy,
She rushed right up to Father, then
Off they waddled to the river.
Tired duckling, home again.

The sea in a shell?

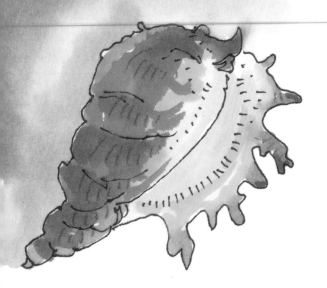

Tom Duckling is sitting on Grandpa Duck's knee. "Look what I've found," says Tom. "Well, I never," says Grandpa, "what a beautiful big shell. That shell is very special." "Really?" says Tom. "Why is it special?" "Well," replies Grandpa, "if you put it up to your ear, you can hear the sea." "Really?" asks Tom. Grandpa nods. Tom picks up the shell and holds it to his ear. Grandpa is right! He can hear the sound of the sea. But that can't be right. The sea is a long way away, isn't it?

July 4

A delicious ice cream

Marie Duckling is sitting at the kitchen table. She is eating ice cream. Not just ordinary ice cream, but four scoops of ice cream in a sundae glass. Each scoop is a different flavor. On the top of the ice cream is a swirl of whipped cream with a cookie in it. On the side is a lovely little parasol. Doesn't it look delicious? Marie takes dainty little mouthfuls. That way her ice cream will last longer!

July 5

Pirate One-Eye

"When I grow up," says Victor Duckling to his friend Thomas, "I'm going to be a pirate." "A pirate?" says Thomas with surprise. "Yes, a pirate," replies Victor. "I'm going to be a pirate on a big ship with three masts. And I'll have an eye patch, because I'll be Pirate One-Eye who sails the world in search of cookies. Everyone will be afraid of me, so they will give me all their cookies and I'll eat them all up." "That sounds good to me," says Thomas. "I think I'll be a pirate too!"

July 6

A big bang

Jet and Oscar Duckling have been given some balloons. They would like to blow them all up, but that's a bit difficult. You have to blow very hard. Father Duck takes a red balloon and begins to blow it up. He blows, and blows, and blows. He blows so hard, and for so long, that the red balloon bursts with a big bang. Father gets quite a fright. Jet and Oscar think it's very funny. Silly Father, he got it all wrong!

July 7

Fire

"Tootaa, tootaa," wails the siren. Daniel and Barbara Duckling look up in surprise.
"Tootaa, tootaa," it goes again. A big red fire engine is coming along the road.
"What do you think has happened?" asks Daniel.
"Come on," says Barbara, "let's go and see."
They run after the fire engine. It stops on the corner. A house is on fire. Big flames are leaping from the roof. The firemen quickly jump out of the fire engine. They have long hoses with water to put out the flames. It doesn't take them long to put out the fire.
"Gosh," says Daniel, "that was exciting. I think I'll be a fire duck when I grow up."
"So will I," says Barbara. "Then we'll put out lots of fires together and be famous!"

July 8

The disappearing duck!

"One fine day,"
Said a little bird,
"Duck got some boots."
Or so he'd heard.

Big red boots,
Duck put them on.
Far too big.
Where's duckling gone?

July 9

A smart life preserver

Otto is at the swimming pool. He isn't very good at swimming, so he's wearing a life preserver. It looks just like a duck. It is around with a hole in the middle. At the front is a head with a beak. When Otto puts it on and gets into the water, he floats quite easily. This means he can have a little rest from swimming every now and again. Isn't that handy?

July 10

The quiet duckling

The Quack family is busy getting ready to go on vacation. Suitcases are packed and the whole house is cleaned. All the family is quacking and chattering. All except one, the smallest duckling, who says nothing.
He says nothing because he can't talk. At least, not yet. However hard he tries, he just can't make a noise. But he is happy that they are going on vacation. They are going to a country where it is lovely and warm.
At last they are ready and they fly away, higher and higher into the sky. It is so peaceful up there above the clouds. Then all of a sudden, a great big monster appears right in front of the little duckling. It is a plane, but the duckling doesn't know that. He gets such a fright that he begins to quack. The plane disappears just as quickly as it appeared.
But everyone is looking at the little duckling. He made a noise! The fright made him talk. Now that he has found his tongue he doesn't stop chattering all of the vacation!

July 11

Camping in the garden

James is on vacation. His tent is in the backyard. It is an excellent
tent, just big enough for James and his duck, Derek. Mother brings them
something to eat and a glass of lemonade every now and then.
James and Derek play games outside the tent, but when it gets dark, they creep into their sleeping bags. James and Derek can't imagine a better vacation than camping in the backyard.
Good night, James. Good night, Derek. Sleep tight!

July 12

Soccer

Melvin and Harold Duckling are playing soccer in the backyard. Melvin kicks the
ball very hard. Harold thinks he can kick it much harder and gives it a great big kick.
Oh dear… The ball goes the wrong way and…crash! It bounces against a window.
The glass shatters into a thousand pieces.
Mother Duck comes straight outside. She is very cross. But Melvin and Harold
didn't break the window on purpose. They help Mother to clear up the broken glass.
Then they go off to play soccer again, this time well away from any windows.

Isn't the hose working?

Mandy and Freddy Duckling are playing in the garden. They are very hot. "I've got a good idea," says Freddy. "Let's get the hose. Then we can spray ourselves with water and we won't be so hot."
He fetches the hose from the shed, attaches it to the tap and turns on the water. But something's wrong. No water comes out. Freddy hasn't noticed that Mandy is squeezing the hose. "I just don't understand," says Freddy. "I've turned on the tap but the water doesn't come out."
"Perhaps there's something blocking it," says Mandy craftily. "Why don't you take a look?"
Freddy looks down the waterhose. "I can't see anything," he says, and gets a jet of water right in the middle of his face. Mandy rolls around on the ground, laughing. But not for long, because Freddy runs over to her and gives her a good soaking too!

July 14

The cold duckling

There once was a duckling
Who was always cold.
He made a fine fire
Of wood dry and old.

He stood near that fire,
Then shouted, "Oh dear,
I've burnt my bottom.
The fire was too near!"

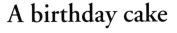

July 15

A birthday cake

Elsie Duckling is in the kitchen. She is helping Mother bake a cake. It is going to be a very special cake – her own birthday cake! Tomorrow is Elsie's birthday.
First they make the cake mixture, then pour it into the cake pan. It goes into the oven to bake, then Mother takes it out again. They decorate it with frosting, and Mother sticks the candles in. It smells delicious.
Elsie would like to try it, but she must wait until tomorrow. She must wait until her birthday.

To the beach

It is lovely weather today. Nick Duckling and his parents are going to the beach. Nick has brought lots of things with him. A bucket, a spade, a fishing net, and a ball. When they get to the beach, Nick and his father make a sandcastle. Then, when they have finished, they have a game of soccer. A bit later they go for a swim. Nick is very tired after all that playing, and falls asleep in the car on the way home. He dreams about the sand, and the sea, and at least a hundred sandcastles!

July 17

A big wave

Jonathon is paddling in the sea. He is holding his cuddly duck. Brr, the water is quite cold, but Jonathon walks out a little further. Then he sees a big wave approaching. Jonathon drops his duck in fright and runs back to the beach. He was just in time. But where is Duck? Jonathon looks around. Then he spots him lying on the sand. The big wave must have thrown him there. Jonathon picks up poor, wet Duck and gives him a cuddle. Perhaps they'll quit swimming for today.

July 18

A goldfish

Leo Duckling has a goldfish. It isn't really made of gold; that's just its name.
Its real color is orange. Leo likes his fish very much. He feeds it every day.
He sprinkles food on the water in the fishbowl. The goldfish knows this,
swims up to the surface and eats the food. Mmm, yummy!

July 19

Swimming trunks with a hole

It is very warm today. All the ducklings
are in the pond. Frank Duckling is
there too. But when Frank gets out
of the water, all the others begin to
laugh. Frank looks himself over.
What are they all laughing at?
Frank doesn't understand. He inspects
himself more thoroughly. Then he
understands. There is a great big hole
in his swimming trunks. Right on his
bottom. He quickly pulls on his clothes
to hide the hole. Mother will have to
buy him a new pair of trunks before
he can go swimming again!

July 20

On the farm

Karen lives on a farm. There are lots of animals on the farm. Cows, sheep, and horses too. And chickens and ducks. Karen likes the ducks best. She gets up early every morning to feed them. She has a big bowl of duck feed and scatters it on the ground. The ducks can't eat it quickly enough. They look so funny. They make Karen laugh.

July 21

The rich duck

I have to tell you
Of a duck in Shoreditch.
He has lots of money,
He's terribly rich.

Each time he has time,
He told me himself,
He goes for a swim
In all his great wealth.

Don't those children speak strangely?

Tina is sitting in the back of the car with her cuddly duck Koko. They are going on vacation to a country far away where it is very hot. It is a long drive before they arrive at the campsite.
Tina goes up to some children playing with a ball and says: "May I play too?" The children answer her, but she doesn't understand a word! Neither does Koko. Don't they sound funny? Tina asks again, but they don't understand each other because they speak different languages.
Tina goes over to the ball, points at it, then points to herself. The other children understand and nod. Tina plays with them until Father comes to fetch her and Koko for supper.
"Bye," says Tina. "See you tomorrow," and waves. The others wave back. So they can understand each other without talking.

Sand pies

Sara Duckling is playing on the beach. She is making pies. Not real pies, sand pies. She puts some sand in a shape, then turns the shape upside down on the sand. She puts some little shells on top of the pies. They look just like little pieces of fruit. The pies look quite real. Almost real enough to eat.

July 24

A castle made of sand

Francis Duckling is playing on the beach with his father. Do you know what they are doing? They are building an enormous castle, a sandcastle. It has four towers and two gates. It looks very good. Francis makes a moat around it. They can put water in that later. Francis and Father do their best to make the castle better and better. When it is finished, they admire their work proudly. Theirs is definitely the best sandcastle on the beach.

July 25

Strange fish

Derek and Barry Duckling are sitting at the edge of the pond. They are fishing, but they haven't caught anything yet. Then Barry's rod begins to move.

"I've got a bite," says Barry, and pulls his rod out of the water. Derek has to help him because it is very heavy. Together they pull the heavy catch out of the pond. But it's not a fish, it's an old shoe! Barry, looks very surprised but Derek just laughs.

"And you thought you had caught a big fish!" laughs Derek. Then his rod begins to wobble. "I've got a bite, too," he says. "Give me a hand."

They pull together on Derek's rod, and this time it isn't a shoe. It's an old boot! "I think we'd better go fish somewhere else," says Barry.

July 26

A big balloon

Wanda and Walter Duckling are lying in the grass enjoying the sun.
"Hey, look over there," says Walter, and points up to the sky.
"What is it?" asks Wanda. "It looks like a big balloon with a basket on it."
"That's right," says Walter, "and there's somebody in the basket."
He begins to shout and waves at the balloon. A duck peers over the edge of
the basket. "Hello, you down there," he shouts, and gives them a wave.
"Gosh, he's flying awfully high," says Wanda. "Isn't he frightened?"
"No, of course not," says Walter, "if you're up high you can see for miles around.
That's what's so good about it." Wanda likes the idea of that, too, but she still
thinks it would be a bit scary. She'd prefer to stay on the ground.

142

The strange duck

I know a strange duckling,
Though beautifully tame.
He thinks only of food
And forgets his own name.

And so if you asked him:
"Pray, what is your name?"
He'd say: "Burger and fries, please,
And you have the same!"

July 28

Just in time!

Harold Duckling is in bed. He is dreaming. In his dream he is bursting to go
to the toilet. He rushes to the bathroom. He almost can't hold it anymore.
At that moment he wakes up, and looks around.
"But I'm in bed," he says, "not in the bathroom." He gets up quickly and runs
to the toilet. Phew, he woke up just in time!
Now that he's out of bed anyway, he goes to the kitchen for a glass of milk.
He was thirsty too.

A hedgehog

Sarah is in the garden playing with her cuddly duck. Suddenly she hears something rustling. The noise is coming from the bushes. Sarah goes over to the bushes to investigate. Carefully she lifts a branch and look, there is a hedgehog. It is looking for food. Sarah rushes into the house to fetch a saucer of milk. She puts it down on the ground in front of the hedgehog. Mmm, it enjoys that. The hedgehog drinks all the milk from the saucer. It was very hungry.

July 30

An arm in a cast

Hans feels a bit sorry for himself. He has broken his arm and it is in a cast, all the way from his wrist to his shoulder. He has to get used to it because he has to do everything with one arm. His plaster arm does look good, though. Everyone has written or drawn something on it. Hans's father drew a duck, a yellow one with an orange beak. So Hans always has something nice to look at.

144

The swimming pool

It is very warm today. The sun is shining brightly and there isn't a cloud to be seen. Leo and Bert Duckling are sitting under a tree. It is a little cooler there. "I know what we'll do," says Leo, "let's make a swimming pool."
"A swimming pool?" asks Bert. "How?"
"We'll dig a hole with a shovel," says Leo, "and when it's big enough, we'll fill it with water." Leo and Bert are just about to start digging when Father Duck arrives.
"What are you two doing?" he asks.
"We're digging a swimming pool," answers Leo.
"Are you nuts?" says Father crossly. "A swimming pool on my lovely lawn? Certainly not. I've a much better idea." Father takes the shovel away with him, but returns with a large, rubber thing. He blows it up. Leo and Bert don't know what he's doing at first, but then they see what it is. It is a swimming pool. They fill it with water and jump in with a great big splash! So they did get a swimming pool after all.

August 1

Annoying Aunt Duck

Wobble Duckling is sitting on the sofa. Aunt Duck is coming to visit. Wobble is not pleased. She always wants to kiss him and she never stops talking. Wobble much prefers playing outside. The telephone rings. Wobble answers it. "Hello," he says.
"Hello, Wobble," says Aunt Duck. "Please tell your mother that I won't be able to come today." "Oh yes, I'll certainly tell her," answers Wobble.
"Good," says Aunt, "and give her my love. Good-bye."
Wobble puts the telephone down and runs to tell Mother that Aunt Duck can't come. Mother is sorry, but Wobble isn't. Now he can go outside to play.

August 2

The duckling with hiccups

I know a duckling
Who lives in a shop.
He got the hiccups
And they wouldn't stop.

Then up jumped a frog,
Upon his head it flopped.
Duckling got a fright
And the hiccups stopped!

A broken leg

Ingrid is down by the pond. She notices a little duck. It is walking rather awkwardly. It can only stand on one leg. Ingrid picks it up very carefully and takes it to the vet. The vet says that the duck's leg is broken. He puts a splint on the broken leg. The duck has to stay at the vet's for a day or two. Ingrid goes to visit the duck every day. He is soon better and Ingrid takes him back to the pond.

August 4

A pond in the garden

At Marianne's house there is a pond in the garden. Lots of fish swim in this pond. Marianne likes looking at the fish. Two ducks visit the pond every day for a swim. Marianne likes to feed them. Her mother gives her some stale bread. She crumbles it and throws it into the pond. The ducks love to eat it. And if they miss any crumbs, the fish gobble those up!

August 5

Making applesauce

Hannah is making applesauce with Grandma. Duck is watching. First they peel lots of apples, then cut them into pieces. They put the pieces into a pan with some water and cook them until they are nice and soft. Then Grandma pushes the cooked apples through a sieve, adds a bit of sugar, and there you are! The applesauce is ready. Hannah and Duck are allowed to taste it. Mmm, delicious!

August 6

I spy with my little eye

It is lovely and warm outside.
Mandy and Freddy Duckling
are lying in the garden.
They are playing a game.
"I spy with my little eye,"
says Mandy, "and it is green."
Freddy has to think about this
one. "Green…" he says,
"I know – grass!"
"Yes," says Mandy, "now it's
your turn."
"I spy with my little eye,"
says Freddy, "and it is yellow."
Mandy thinks about it.
She doesn't know the answer.
"It is yellow," says Freddy,
"and around and it's in the sky."
Mandy still doesn't know.
Can you guess what
Freddy means?

August 7

In the baby buggy

Sandra has a new baby brother.
He is still very tiny. He sleeps in his
cradle most of the time. But today
Sandra is taking him out for a walk.
Mother puts him into the baby buggy
and Sandra is allowed to push. Sandra
has put her toy duck in the buggy, too.
Duck is lying nice and close to the
baby. They go for a walk in the park.
Sandra is very proud of her baby
brother. So is Duck.

August 8

Close together

Can you see that duckling
Lying next to Baby?
Whatever is he doing there?
I'm going to ask. Well, maybe.

"Duckling, duckling, tell me.
Why are you lying there?"
"I'm close to little brother.
His buggy I may share."

August 9

Driving a car

It is Peter's birthday today. Mother and Father have given him a beautiful present. When he woke up this morning, there was a red go-cart next to his bed, with a big red bow around it. It looks like a real car. Father has put the go-cart out in the garden. Peter puts his toy duck in the back and gets in the driver's seat. He begins to pedal and drives around and around the garden. He's just like a racing driver. Peter goes so fast that poor Duck nearly falls off.

August 10

A fun day after all!

Winnie and Sonny Duckling live with their father and mother by the duck pond. It is Sunday. Winnie and Sonny are bored. They don't feel like playing tag or marbles or anything. What are they going to do?
Father and Mother have a good idea.
They could go to the playground! Hurray!
Winnie and Sonny go on the swings and the seesaw. They whoosh down the slide and clamber on the junglegym. They really enjoy themselves.
And they get an ice cream too!
So it was a fun day after all!

Becoming famous

Thomas Duckling is practicing. He is practicing his violin. It is very difficult to play the violin. Thomas practices every day. When he is grown up, he wants to be a famous violinist. So famous that everyone would have heard of him. He will have to practice very hard if he wants to become famous. Who knows, he might become one of the most famous ducks in the world!

A drawing for Grandma

Joanna is sitting at the table. She is doing a drawing for Grandma, who is ill. Joanna is doing her very best drawing. She draws a big pond with a duck in it. It is a very big duck. Ducks are quite hard to draw. When she has finished she takes the drawing to Grandma. Grandma thinks it's lovely. In fact, it has made her feel a bit better already.

August 13

Learning to fly

Mother Duck is swimming in the stream. Four ducklings are swimming along behind her. Today she is going to teach them to fly. Mother shows them.
She stretches her wings and flaps them up and down.
The four ducklings copy her, but nothing happens. Then they flap their wings much quicker and yes, off they go. One by one they fly up into the sky.
Aren't they clever?

August 14

The duckling from Skye

I know of a duckling
Who lives in Skye.
His mother has only just
Taught him how to fly.

But something is wrong,
That duckling is a clown.
You wouldn't believe it,
But he flies upside down!

A bit lost

Jake is shopping in town with his mother. He has brought his toy duck Snicks with him. They go into a big store that sells everything. Clothes, shoes, lots more things and, best of all, toys. Jake and Snicks go to look at the games. What a lot there are! Then they move on to the cuddly toys. There is an enormous elephant. "Mother, look at this huge elephant," says Jake. But Mother doesn't answer. Mother is not standing behind Jake. Jake can't find her anywhere. He feels a bit frightened. Where could Mother be? He begins to cry and hugs Snicks tight. A salesclerk comes up to him. She realizes right away what is the matter. She takes Jake and Snicks to a special corner with a microphone. They make an announcement through the microphone that Jake has lost his mother. Mother comes in no time. She had been very worried. Jake and Snicks are very happy to see Mother, and they stop crying. From then on Jake holds Mother's hand very tightly when they are walking around the store. He doesn't want to lose her again!

August 16

Shadow?

Tim and Tom Duckling are playing outside.
The sun is shining and there isn't a cloud to
be seen. "Hey, that's funny," says Tim
suddenly, "there's a black mark on the ground
there. If I stand still it doesn't move, but if I
move it moves too! Whatever is it?"
Tom laughs. "Silly, that's your shadow!"
"My shadow?" says Tim with surprise.
"Yes," replies Tom, "everything has a shadow.
From the light of the sun. The sun shines on
you, but you block some light that would
have shone on the ground. That makes the
black mark that we call a shadow."
Tim thinks it's a strange story. He doesn't
really believe it. Do you?

August 17

Still small

Jimmy Duckling lives by the pond in the wood with his mother, father and at least ten
brother and sister ducklings. But all the brother and sister ducklings are bigger than
Jimmy. He is the youngest and the smallest. He doesn't always like being the youngest
and the smallest, because the others boss him about. So Jimmy often dreams about
when he will be as big as the other ducklings. Then he will be able to do as he pleases.
He can hardly wait!

A strange string

Jonas is in the bath. The bath is full of ducks.
Yellow ducks specially for bathtime.
Then Jonas notices a strange piece
of string on the bottom of the bath.
What could it be? Jonas gives it a pull.
There's a round, black thing on the end of it.
Very odd. But what's happening?
It looks like all the water is running
out of the bath. It is, because Jonas has
pulled the plug out!

August 19

Good friends

Will Duckling has a dog. The dog is brown and very well behaved. He is called Flip.
Will takes him for a walk every day three times a day. Sometimes Will puts Flip on
a leash, but he lets him loose so that he can have a good run about, too. Will throws
a stick into the air for Flip to catch. They play other games too. They love playing
together, because they are very good friends.

156

August 20

The duckling from Harrow

I know a duckling
Who lives in Harrow.
He keeps on trying
To catch his shadow.

But whatever he does,
Jump, sit, or stand,
His shadow he never
Can catch in his hand.

August 21

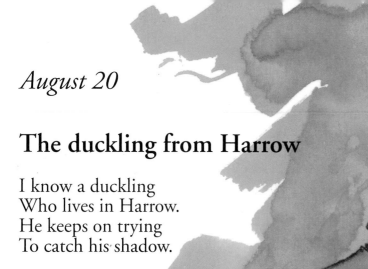

Lovely slippers

Anna has new slippers. They are not just ordinary slippers, they are duck slippers!
They are brown with wings on the sides. On the front is an orange beak with two eyes
above it. The duck slippers look really lovely and keep Anna's feet nice and warm.
She is very pleased with them. She calls them her cuddly slippers.

August 22

Looking at the stars

Mario Duckling is in bed, but he can't get to sleep. It is very late and very dark outside. Then Mario has an idea. He gets out of bed, opens the curtains and sits on the windowsill. There are shiny lights in the sky. Those are the stars. There are lots of them. The moon is there too. Mario enjoys looking at the stars. When he has finished looking he goes back to bed. He dreams about the stars shining brightly in the sky. Sleep well, Mario. See you in the morning.

August 23

A diving board

It is very warm outside. Simon and Thomas Duckling are swimming in the pond. "I know what we can do," says Thomas. "See that tree over there? We'll climb it and jump off into the water." Simon thinks it's a good idea. They climb the tree together. Thomas leaps off a branch into the water with a big splash. Simon follows. What fun! They've found themselves a diving board!

August 24

A small boat

Eddie and Robin Duckling have made a small boat. It is made of wood and has a little mast. There are two sails on the mast. Eddie and Robin don't yet know if the boat will float. So they have brought it to the stream to try it out.
Eddie puts it onto the water. Yes, it floats! It was a good idea to have tied a piece of string to the boat too, so it can't sail away all by itself now, can it?

August 25

Antoinette Duckling

Antoinette Duckling,
Now fancy that.
Well, one day
She put on a hat!

The day was windy,
Windy as can be,
And that old wind thought:
Give that hat to me!

So if you see a hat
High up in the sky,
You'll know how it got there,
Whose it is, and why!

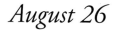

August 26

Real Indians?

Ferdy and Micky Duckling are wearing dress-up clothes. They are wearing Indian costumes with feather headdresses. They both have bows and quivers filled with arrows on their backs. They whoop and shout and wave their bows and arrows as they run about. They look so real that they almost make you frightened.

August 27

A lovely prize

Walt has won a prize in a coloring competition. He colored in a picture very beautifully and then sent it in. Lots of others did that as well. Some grown-ups chose the coloring they liked best, and it was Walt's. So Walt won the prize. Do you know what it is? It is a very big cup with a big number 1 on it. Walt is very pleased with his prize.

August 28

Elf soup

Ernest and Victor Duckling are playing in the garden. They have a bowl of water and are putting things in it. They are looking for daisies and dandelions, berries and duckweed. They are being very secretive.
Mother comes out to see what they are doing.
"What are you two doing?" she asks.
"We're making soup," says Ernest.
"Soup?" says Mother with surprise.
"Yes," says Victor, "real soup."
"What sort of soup?" Mother wants to know.
"We're not telling," says Ernest.
But Victor can't keep a secret and says: "It's elf soup."
"Elf soup?" says Mother. "I've never heard of that. Who is going to eat it?"
"The elves, of course," says Ernest. "We can't eat it, because it would make us ill. The soup is specially for the elves."
Ernest and Victor carry on stirring their elf soup. Mother doesn't understand, but mothers don't need to know everything, do they?

August 29

A magician at school

There is a party today at Karl's school. The children don't have to do any writing or arithmetic. They are allowed to play games all day. A magician is coming too. A magician is someone who can do funny and clever tricks. He wears very smart clothes – a black cape and a black top hat. He conjures a duck out of the hat for one of his tricks. Karl thinks he is so clever that he decides to become a magician himself when he is grown up.

August 30

A duck out of a hat

Wait a minute,
Can it be that?
A duck inside
A black top hat!

Yes, I'm right.
Well, well, well.
Expected a rabbit –
You never can tell!

August 31

Peas everywhere

Mandy and Freddy Duckling are sitting at the table. They are eating green peas
and spinach. "How may peas have you got?" asks Mandy.
"Let me count," replies Freddy, "one, two, three, four…twelve. I've got twelve.
What about you?" "I've got eleven," says Mandy.
"I know a good game," says Freddy. "You have to throw as many peas in the sink
as you can. But you have to do it with your spoon, not your hands."
"Okay," says Mandy, and puts a pea on her spoon. She throws the pea over to the sink,
but the pea was not alone on her spoon. There was some spinach there, too, and it
makes a big, green splotch on the kitchen cupboard.
Mandy and Freddy aren't worried about it. They just keep throwing peas and spinach
around the kitchen. Then Mother comes into the room.
She is extremely annoyed. Mother gives them a good talking-to, then sends them to
their bedrooms. No more peas for them. And no more silly games either.

September 1

First day at school

Barry is going to school for the first time today. He is a bit scared. So Mother has said that he may take his cuddly duck Quacky with him. When Barry is at school, Quacky sits on his knee. Barry holds Quacky very tight, because there are lots of children he doesn't know. He doesn't know the teacher either. But he gets to know them all quite quickly, and then school doesn't seem as scary anymore. In fact, Barry is going to leave Quacky at home tomorrow, because he feels brave enough to go on his own.

September 2

A sunflower

Willy Duckling is in the garden with Grandpa. They notice a great big flower.
It has a tall, thick stem with big, green leaves on it. The flower is right at the top.
The middle of the flower is brown with yellow petals around the edge.
"What kind of flower is it?" asks Willy.
"It is a sunflower," answers Grandpa. "It's called a sunflower because it looks like the sun." Willy thinks that's a funny name. The flower does look a bit like the sun, but the sun isn't brown in the middle, is it?

September 3

At the market

"Fish, fresh fish, lovely fresh fish today!" shouts the fishmonger at the market.
He keeps on shouting, telling everyone about his lovely fresh fish, and it works.
Lots of people crowd around his stall. There is another crowd at the back of his stall,
a crowd of ducks. Do you know why they're there? To eat the scraps of fish the
fishmonger throws away when he cleans the fish. They're having a lovely time.
They begin to quack because they are enjoying themselves, until the fishmonger
notices them. "Away with all of you!" he shouts. "Get out from under my feet!
Go on back to the pond!" The ducks flap about in a panic. No more fish
for them today. But it's not so bad, because they had managed to eat
lots of fish before the fishmonger noticed them.

Upside down

"Can you stand on your head?" Mandy Duckling asks Freddy Duckling.
"Of course I can," replies Freddy, "look!" He stands on his head.
"So can I," says Mandy, and she stands on her head too.
Both of them have to try very hard not to lose their balance and fall over.
"Doesn't everything look funny?" says Mandy. "Everything is upside down."
"Yes, an upside-down world," says Freddy. They stand on their heads for a bit longer because they think everything looks so funny.

September 5

A redhead

I've something to tell
Of a redheaded duck.
Believe me, I've seen it
(It's not just bad luck.)

He doesn't stand straight.
No, he stands on his head
Seven days at a time,
So no wonder he's red!

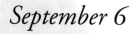

A very nice pen

Rupert is writing with a very nice
pen. Rupert made the pen himself.
He made it from a duck's feather.
A pen like this is called a quill pen.
Rupert found the feather by the
duck pond and brought it home.
He took the inside out of another
pen and put it in the feather. This
made a new pen from an old feather.
Rupert is going to take the pen with
him to school tomorrow.
Perhaps the teacher will ask
him to make a duck feather
pen for her too!

September 7

Duck pajamas

It was Leo's birthday yesterday. He got
a great present. A new pair of pajamas. Not
just ordinary pajamas, pajamas with ducks
on them. Big ducks, little ducks, fat ducks
and thin ducks. Leo is very proud of his
pajamas. They are the nicest pajamas he
has ever had. He's sure he will sleep
well in them. Night night, Leo.
Night night, duck pajamas.
See you in the morning.

September 8

What funny dandelions

Marie Duckling is in the garden. She is
looking for dandelions. But something is
rather strange. The dandelions had lovely
yellow petals, so they were easy to recognize.
But now the petals are gone, and instead
there are white, fluffy balls. Marie doesn't
understand. She picks one and takes it
to show Mother.
Mother tells her that dandelions change.
When the flowers die, the yellow petals fall
off and are replaced by seeds. The seeds are
the black things on the end of the white,
fluffy things.
Then Mother blows the white, fluffy bits
and they float away. They are like tiny
parachutes carrying the seed with them.
And wherever the seed lands, a new
dandelion plant will grow.

September 9

Gertie is cross

Gertie, Jasper's toy duck, is sitting outside in a corner. She looks very unhappy. She is cross because Jasper has left her outside. Jasper went inside to play and forgot all about her. Gertie wanted to play inside too. That's why she looks so cross. She doesn't like sitting outside on her own one little bit. She feels something on her head. Raindrops. Oh no, it's raining! But here comes Jasper. He didn't really forget about Gertie. Now they can play together again. Inside.

September 10

Feathers everywhere

Tim and Tom Duckling are having a pillow fight. They both have a pillow and are hitting them against each other. But they hit them so hard that one of the pillows bursts. A great cloud of feathers comes out. Tim and Tom are a bit taken aback, but they giggle nervously since it is quite funny. Mother Duck, who comes in at that moment, is not amused. She is cross. Tim and Tom have to clear up all the mess and promise never to do it again.

September 11

That's difficult!

"Look at this," says Tom to his friend Kooky Duckling. "There's a funny little
insect and it's making a complicated pattern with a lot of threads."
Kooky comes to look. "That's a spider," he says, "and he's spinning a web."
A spider and a web? Tom doesn't understand. Kooky tries to explain.
"A spider is an insect with eight legs. It likes to eat small flies. To catch the flies,
it builds a web. The flies fly into the web and get stuck. Then along comes
the spider and eats them up! Just like that."
"Yuck," says Tom, and makes a face. "I wouldn't want to eat flies! And I'm sure
I couldn't make a web from all those sticky threads. Far too difficult.
I think I'll leave it to the spider."

The duckling from London town

I met a duckling
In London town.
He had on his beak
A ribbon, tied around.

I asked him: "Why
The bow on your beak?"
He didn't answer
For he couldn't speak!

Fishing with a shovel?

"Are you coming fishing?" Jacob Duckling asks his friend Elly.
"Yes, I am," answers Elly, "though I've never done it before."
"Okay," says Jacob, "here's the shovel."
"Going fishing with a shovel?" says Elly with surprise.
"No, silly," says Jacob, "the shovel is to dig up the worms with."
"Worms?" asks Elly, "what do we need them for?" She makes a face.
"Well," says Jacob, "fish like eating worms."
"Yuck," says Elly, "how could anyone possibly like eating those
horrid, slimy, wriggly things? I don't think I'll go with you after all.
I'll come and see how you're doing a bit later."

September 14

Rhyming

"Can you rhyme?" Hans Duckling asks his
friend Jeremy. "Rhyme?" says Jeremy,
"I've never heard of it. What does it mean?"
"Rhymes are words that sound like each other.
Grass rhymes with *brass*."
"Oh, I see," says Jeremy. "Can you think of
another rhyme?" Hans thinks for a moment,
then says: "*Poo* rhymes with *shoe*," and
dissolves into giggles. "Oh, now I get it,"
says Jeremy. "I've got one too. *Wee* rhymes
with *tree*!" Both of them burst out laughing.
Can you think of a good rhyme?

September 15

Toy clothes

Jo has a toy duck. It is a lovely soft, cuddly duck. Jo has special clothes for her duck.
They are in a suitcase. There is a pair of pants, a sweater, and some pajamas.
When Jo puts her pajamas on to go to bed at night, Duck gets his pajamas on too.
Then they both go to sleep. Jo and Duck in their pajamas. Night night, both of you.

September 16

Duck wallpaper

Nick has a very special bedroom. He has a bed and some toys. Nothing special about that. Can you guess what is so special? The wallpaper. It is duck wallpaper. The walls are covered in all sorts of different ducks. Big ones, small ones, fat and thin ones, brown, yellow, blue, and even purple ducks!
When Nick goes to bed at night, he looks at all his ducks. He keeps on seeing ones he hasn't seen before. There are just so many of them.

September 17

If I were king

Said Keith the duckling:
"If I were king,
I'd be the boss
Of everything."

"I'd eat ice cream
And fries all day.
Send everyone home
For a vacation."

A pond outside the house

There is a big pond outside Eric's house. First the workmen dug a big hole, then they filled it with water. Do you know what Eric likes best about the pond? The ducks that come there every day. There must be about ten of them. Eric loves watching the ducks. Sometimes he throws some stale bread in the pond for them to eat. Isn't Eric lucky having a duck pond outside his house? I wish I had one.

September 19

A green head

Toby is at the pond with Grandpa. Ducks are swimming in the water. "Grandpa," asks Toby, "why is that duck gray with a green head and the other duck all white?" "Well," says Grandpa, "that is because the duck with the green head is a male duck – a drake – and the other is a female duck." "Really?" says Toby with surprise. "I didn't know that. It's lucky we aren't ducks, isn't it, Grandpa?" "Why's that?" asks Grandpa. "Why, then you and I and Father would all have to have green heads!" laughs Toby.

175

September 20

A funny mirror

Gerard Duckling is at the fair. He has already been on a merry-go-round and some other rides. Walking along, he sees a mirror. He looks at himself in it. He looks very odd. In his reflection he has a fat tummy and a great big head. Gerard feels his head and his tummy to see if they feel bigger. No, they feel just the same as always. Then he looks again in the mirror. His tummy and head still look huge. What can be the matter? A fairground attendant just happens to be passing. "They're fun, aren't they, the distorting mirrors?" he says. "Distorting mirrors?" says Gerard with surprise. "I thought they were just ordinary mirrors." "No, silly," says the man, "these are very special mirrors. When you look at yourself in them, you look funny – all distorted. That's why they're called distorting mirrors." "Oh, good," sighs Gerard with relief. "I was beginning to think I really looked like that!"

September 21

The scrapbook

Lisa collects ducks. Not real ducks, pictures of ducks, which she cuts out. She sticks them all in a scrapbook. Her scrapbook is almost full. There are only a few empty pages left. Each year on her birthday, Lisa is given some more pictures of ducks for her scrapbook. She keeps on sticking them in her scrapbook until it is full. It is fun to look through Lisa's scrapbook. It is full of all different sorts of ducks. I didn't know there were quite so many different kinds.

September 22

Grandma knits

Grandma Duck is sitting on the sofa. She is knitting. "What are you knitting?" asks Hilda Duckling. "A sweater," answers Grandma. "Is that difficult?" asks Hilda. "Not really," says Grandma. "Look, I'll show you." She puts the needle through the wool, wraps the other end of the wool around the needle and pulls it through. Lots and lots of times. Hilda doesn't understand at all. It looks very complicated. "I think knitting is still a bit too difficult for me," she says. "I'm going outside to play. Bye, Grandma."

The duckling who liked to swim

There once was a duckling
Who liked to swim.
He lived on a pond,
Wasn't happy, not him.

So he packed his case,
With some clothes and a book.
Now he lives on a pond
Close to me. Come and look.

September 24

I prefer lemonade

Father and Mother Duck are having a cup of coffee. "May I have some coffee too?" asks Lucas Duckling. "Do you like coffee?" asks Mother. "I don't know," answers Lucas, "but I'd like to try some." Mother pours a cup of coffee for Lucas. He adds milk and sugar, then stirs it. He takes a mouthful, then makes a face. "Yuck," he says, "coffee isn't as nice as I thought. I think I want a glass of lemonade." Mother smiles.

178

Bruno the dog

Vera has a dog called Bruno.
Bruno is a very unusual dog.
He has his own toy duck.
He often plays with his duck,
and when he goes to sleep, his
duck is there beside him in his
basket. When Vera takes Bruno
for a walk, Duck goes along too.
Bruno carries Duck in his
mouth. He is very careful
not to hurt him. A dog
with a toy duck in his mouth.
What a funny sight!

Hustle bustle

Boris and Victor Duckling are out on a long walk through the wood. They are a bit
tired and look for somewhere to sit down. Boris is about to sit on a hump of earth
when Victor shouts out: "No, don't sit there!" Boris is startled. "Why not?" he asks.
"That's no ordinary hump of earth, that's an anthill," explains Victor. Boris looks at
the hump with surprise. "Yes, I see what you mean," he says, "there are ants running
everywhere. What a big house they have." "They're making it even bigger," says Victor.
"Can you see how they run to and fro carrying things all the time?" "What a hustle
bustle," says Boris. "It makes me tired just watching them."

179

I want to be a doctor

Ian wants to be a doctor when he grows up. He would like to learn how to make people better. He practices on his toy duck. He pretends that Duck has broken his leg and bandages it. If Duck has a cold, Ian checks his temperature with a thermometer.
I think Ian will make a very good doctor when he is bigger.
At least he will have had years of practice.

September 28

In the stroller

Pauline is out for a walk. She has taken her stroller with her. Do you know who is sitting in the stroller? Pauline's toy duck. He's nice and warm under a blanket. He's having a good rest and really enjoying his little trip. He likes being out with Pauline too.

September 29

A clever old duck

Once I saw an old duck
Who lived in Timbuktu.
He spoke seven languages,
Was good at drawing too.

He was very, very old,
One hundred years or more.
Such an old and clever duck
I've never seen before.

September 30

Let's pretend

Marie and Bob are playing mothers and fathers. Snicks, the toy duck, is their baby.
Marie and Bob are having a cup of tea and Snicks is having a bottle. Snicks is sitting
on Marie's knee. When the bottle is finished, Bob takes Snicks up to bed.
Bob reads him a story too. Then they all go to sleep.
Marie and Bob are just like a real father and mother. They're very good at playing
let's pretend. But they get tired of it after a while, so they go outside to play.

October 1

Fun in the rain

It is raining heavily. Great big drops of rain are falling from the sky. All the ducks are inside. All except Rick Duckling. Rick is swimming in the pond. He likes swimming in the rain. He gets wet when he's swimming anyway. And when he swims in the rain, it's as if he's in the shower. An outside shower!

October 2

Just like a mirror

Bert Duckling is out for a walk. There are big puddles everywhere since it has just stopped raining. Bert looks into a big puddle. Hey, who's that? He sees the face of a duck in the puddle. The face looks remarkably like his own face. Bert sticks his tongue out. So does the face in the puddle. Then Bert realizes what's happening. The face in the puddle is his own face. The puddle is just like a mirror.

A special towel

Francis is in the bathtub. He is getting washed. When he is nice and clean, he gets out of the bathtub. Mother gets a big towel to dry Francis. It is a very special towel. There is a picture of a duck on it. The towel is so big that you can hardly see Francis when he is wrapped up in it. All you can see is the duck.

October 4

Animal day

Today is a sort of vacation. It is animal day. Hugo looks after the animals on the farm. He gives the cows and sheep some extra food today. The dogs and cats get some extra tasty morsels too. Hugo always looks after the animals well, but he tries even harder today. He even remembers the ducks on the stream behind the farm. He has a big bag of bread for them. Mmm, they'll enjoy that! The ducks all hurry up and swim toward Hugo when they see him coming with such a big bag full of bread.

October 5

To the sun

I know a stubborn duckling
Who set off for the sun.
It was a silly thing to do.
Too far, too hot, no fun.

When he was only halfway,
That silly duck turned back.
He said the sun was far too hot
And it had burnt his back.

October 6

A tear in Theo's jacket

Theo wants to go and stroke the ducks sleeping in the field. But to get into the field he must go under some barbed wire. Barbed wire is wire with sharp points on it. Theo creeps carefully under the barbed wire, but not carefully enough. His jacket gets caught, and, as Theo tries to pull it free, it tears. Oh dear, now Theo will have to go home and tell Mother. He gives the ducks a quick pat, then runs home. Mother isn't too cross, and she says she can mend his jacket. But Theo has to promise her that he will never creep under any barbed wire again.

In the rowboat

Bob and his father are in the rowboat. They are going rowing. Duck is with them, too. Bob and Father are sitting in the middle of the boat. That's where the oars are fixed to the boat. You have to be strong to row, but Bob is very good at it. Duck sits on the prow of the boat. He's keeping a lookout. Now and then he waves at some real ducks that swim by. Ahoy there!

October 8

A mechanical duck

"It works, it works!" cries Astrid. "Look, it's walking!" Mother comes to look. Astrid has been given a lovely duck. Not a real one, but not a cuddly duck either. The duck is made of metal, and there is a key in its side. You turn the key and wind it up. When it is wound up, it walks. It waddles around the living room taking tiny steps. It looks almost real.

A silly seagull

William is out walking on the beach with
his mother and father. It is very windy and
there are high waves. Lovely to look at.
William has brought his cuddly duck
with him. Together they look up at the
seagulls, floating high on the wind.
Suddenly something falls from the sky.
It lands right on Duck's head. Can you
guess what it is? Seagull poo!
William quickly wipes it off. William
and Duck glare at the seagulls.
How could they do such a thing!

October 10

The duckling from
Paddington

I know a duckling
Who lives in Paddington.
He goes around all day
Kissing everyone.

His father and his mother
He never ever misses.
Also his brother, sister too,
He showers them with kisses!

October 11

Swimming in a flowerpot

It has been raining heavily. The garden is full of puddles. Dennis is looking out of the window. He would like to go outside to play. But he doesn't know what to do. The grass will be far too wet for a game of soccer.

Then Dennis gets an idea. He notices a big flowerpot full of water. It looks like a little pond. He runs to Mother and asks: "May I take my plastic duck outside? I'm going to let it swim in the big flowerpot!"

"That's fine," says Mother, "but only if you put your blue boots on. There are so many puddles in the garden." Dennis fetches the duck, puts his boots and his coat on and goes outside. The plastic duck has a fine time swimming in the flowerpot. He was a bit bored with swimming in the bath.

October 12

On Father's shoulders

When Henry goes for a walk with his parents, Father sometimes lets him sit on his shoulders. Henry is then up high and can see everything. Henry has a toy duck who sometimes is allowed to go out for a walk with them. Henry sits him on Father's head. Duck gets a good view of everything, just like Henry. And they don't have to walk, so they don't get tired. Poor Father gets a bit tired, though.

October 13

Ducks on the window

Nell is in the car. She is going to visit Grandma with Father and Mother. Nell usually gets bored in the car, but not today. Nell has been given some stickers. Special stickers for the window. One of the stickers is of a big duck, another is of a little duck, and there are lots more. By the time Nell has stuck them all on the window, they are already at Grandma's house. Doesn't time fly?

October 14

A snail with a house

"Hey, look over here," says Mandy to Freddy Duckling. "Look at that, on the ground there. What is it?" "That is a snail," says Freddy. "I know that," says Mandy, "but what is that on its back?" "That's its house," says Freddy. "Its house?" says Mandy with surprise. "Why would anyone take their house out for a walk?" "Snails do it all the time," says Freddy, "and its really quite handy. If it gets tired, all it has to do is creep back into its shell for a snooze." Mandy agrees that it is handy, but she still thinks it's a bit strange.

October 15

A present with a bow

"What a big present,"
Said Joe the Duck.
"I'll just undo this bow
And look, look, look!"

He fiddled and he fiddled,
The bow was tight, you know.
But still he hasn't managed
To undo that bow!

October 16

Magic?

Father Duck is sitting on the sofa reading the newspaper. There is a cup of coffee and a plate of cakes on the table. Father drinks a mouthful of coffee and takes a bite of cake. Then he puts the rest of his cake on the saucer and keeps reading the newspaper. What Father doesn't know is that Wobble Duckling is hiding under the table. Very quietly he takes the cake from the saucer. Father doesn't notice.
"Hey," says Father, "where's my cake gone?" He doesn't understand. He looks around the room, then takes another cake. He takes a bite, then puts the rest down on the saucer as before. Wobble takes this cake, too, and again Father doesn't notice.
"I'm quite sure I put my cake down on that saucer," says Father a little later, "and now it's gone again. It must be magic. I don't understand it at all!" He shakes his head. We know what has happened, don't we? But ssh, you won't tell, will you?

191

Kooky runs away

Kooky Duckling has run away from home. He doesn't like it there anymore.
His big brother keeps teasing him and making him unhappy.
It gets dark very quickly in the wood. Kooky is a bit cold and very hungry.
They will be having supper at home now.
Kooky changes his mind. There are lots of nice things at home too.
So he turns around and runs home as fast as he can.

October 18

New boots

Billy Duckling has a new pair of boots.
They are lovely green boots. Do you know
why Billy is so pleased with his new boots?
Because he will be able to splash through
the puddles in them after it has rained.
He'll jump from one puddle to the next,
and it won't matter one bit because
his feet won't get wet!

Absolutely nothing

"Look, over there by that tree," says Jonnie Duckling to his friend Walter.
They go over to see what is lying there. "It is a chest," says Walter.
"Perhaps it's a treasure chest. It might be full of gold or candy."
"Shall we open it?" asks Jonnie. Walter thinks they should. So they open
the chest and what do you think they find in it? Absolutely nothing!
"Oh, what a shame," says Jonnie, "I really hoped there would be something
good in it." Jonnie and Walter go off in search of something more exciting.

October 20

The secret

There once was a duck
Who had a big trunk.
What was in there?
Maybe junk!

Maybe gold or chocolate,
Or a bike to ride.
But no one ever
Got to look inside!

October 21

A walking dish towel

Richard has a real duck called Frances as a pet. Frances lives outside in the summer. But now that it's getting colder, Frances is allowed into the kitchen. Do you know what she does? She creeps under a dish towel to keep warm and have a sleep. But when she wakes up, sometimes she doesn't remember where she is. Then she runs about with the dish towel still on top of her. This really makes Richard laugh. A dish towel with legs is quite a funny sight.

October 22

A duck mug

Yuri is in the kitchen. Mother has made him some chocolate milk. Yummy. It tastes twice as good because the chocolate milk is in Yuri's special mug. It is a duck mug, with Yuri's name on one side. That way no one can forget that the duck mug is Yuri's. And no one else is allowed to drink out of Yuri's duck mug.

October 23

Looking for horse chestnuts

Mandy and Freddy Duckling are in the wood looking for bright, shiny horse chestnuts. There are lots lying on the ground. "Hey," says Mandy, "this is funny. It's green, around, and prickly." She shows the funny thing to Freddy. "That's a horse chestnut too," he says. "But it's not brown and it's certainly not smooth," says Mandy. "No," replies Freddy, "the green bit is the skin of the horse chestnut. Look." He picks the skin off. Inside there is a beautiful, shiny brown horse chestnut. Mandy didn't know that. They keep collecting chestnuts until they have lots and lots.

October 24

A drawing on the window

It is cold and raining outside. Otto is bored. He presses his nose up against the window. He looks at the raindrops falling. His breath makes a cloud on the window. Hey, he thinks, now I can do a drawing. Otto draws a duck on the window. A big, beautiful duck. Otto completely forgets that he was bored and covers the window with drawings.

195

Lucy Duckling

Do you know Lucy Duckling?
She lives in the city,
And all she ever does
Is make herself pretty.

Some lipstick here,
Some gel in her hair.
She's busy all day.
She makes people stare.

October 26

Making dolls

Tim and Tom Duckling are sitting at the kitchen table. On the table there are acorns, lots of acorns. Tim and Tom are making acorn dolls.
First they take a big acorn. This is for the tummy. They stick toothpicks in it for legs and arms, then put another, smaller acorn on with another toothpick for the head. Tim and Tom have made lots of acorn dolls. They're having great fun.

Storm

Pip is in bed. There is a storm outside. The wind whistles through the roof tiles and the branches of the big tree in front of the house sway back and forth. It is raining heavily too. It is a really good storm. Pip isn't worried. He has crept right down under the covers with his cuddly duck. They snuggle close to each other. Down there under the covers you would hardly know that there was a storm outside. Night night, Pip. Night night, Duck. Sweet dreams.

October 28

The naughty wind!

It is now well into autumn and there are lots of leaves on the ground. Stuart Duckling is helping Father tidy up the leaves in the garden. Stuart has a big rake and is raking all the leaves into a pile. He has already raked a big pile together.
But oh dear. There is a great gust of wind. The wind blows the leaves right back all over the garden. Stuart must start all over again. Stuart is annoyed and waves his rake at the wind. That won't help much, but it does make Stuart feel a bit better.

October 29

A duck house

Joshua is in the shed with his father. They are making a house for the winter. Not a house for the birds, but a house for the ducks. Two ducks come into Joshua's garden every day. In the summer, Joshua feeds them bread, but in the winter there is sometimes snow on the ground and it often rains. So Joshua decides to make a duck house to put the bread in. Then the ducks will be able to eat without getting wet.

October 30

Warm and dry

It's terribly cold
With rain and storm.
But a duck house keeps
Them nice and warm.

It's cozy inside,
No snow, no ice,
And plenty of bread.
Now isn't that nice?

October 31

Duckweed

Edward and Heather are playing in a field. They are playing tag.
"You're it," shouts Edward and runs away very fast. Heather runs after him.
Suddenly she shouts: "Look out, there's…" But it's too late. Edward was running so fast that he didn't see the stream covered with duckweed. Duckweed is as green as grass, and if it covers the water you really can't see that there's water underneath. Luckily the stream isn't deep. A couple of ducks in the stream did get a fright. They were quietly nibbling some duckweed when all of a sudden a boy falls into the water right in front of their beaks. Edward climbs out of the stream as quickly as he can. Heather just has to laugh. Edward does look so funny covered in duckweed. It's everywhere, in his hair, on his arms and legs, everywhere. He'll have to go home and have a shower to clean himself up. Poor Edward.

Very well hidden

Tim and Tom are playing hide-and-seek in the wood. Tom is hiding and Tim must find him. Tim counts to ten. There are lots of leaves on the ground because it is autumn. Tom sees all the leaves and has an idea: he creeps under a pile of leaves. You can hardly see him, he is so well hidden. You can just see his tail sticking out above the leaves. Tim has finished counting. He looks around, then looks behind the trees and among the bushes. He searches and searches, but can't find Tom anywhere. Where could he be? Tim gives up. "I give up," he says, "come out now!" The leaves on the ground begin to rustle and out pops Tom.
Hadn't he found an excellent hiding place?

Our own names

"Grandpa," says Yuri Duckling, "have you got a name?"
"Oh yes," says Grandpa. "My name is William."
"Why do we have names?" asks Yuri.
Grandpa laughs and says: "Well, wouldn't it be a bit complicated if we didn't have names? Just imagine it. Someone calls out: Duck, come here. All the ducks would turn around, but no one would know who was being called."
"I see what you mean," says Yuri, "so having our own names is a good idea after all."

Unusual earrings

Jasmin was given some lovely earrings for her birthday. They're not ordinary earrings. They are duck earrings. They are quite small and have their own little box. Jasmin doesn't wear them every day. She wears them on special days. It looks as if two tiny ducks are dangling from her ears. They sparkle a little as Jasmin turns her head. The duck earrings really do look lovely.

Lots of bubbles

Martin is in the bath with his ducks. There are lots of bubbles floating on the water. Martin decides he wants some more. He gets the bottle of bubble bath to squirt a bit more into the water. But oh dear, he drops the bottle. He tries to get hold of it again, but it is too slippery. All that swishing through the water makes even more bubbles. So many bubbles, in fact, that you can't see Martin at all. All you can see are the ducks floating on the top.

November 5

The interesting duck

There once was a duck,
Who was interesting.
Guess what? That duck
Always lost everything.

His mother said to him:
"Remember what I say,
Remember where you put things,
Every single day."

That didn't help at all.
He forgot what Mother said.
I'm sure if it was loose,
He'd go and lose his head!

November 6

A real slide

Bert has thought up a good game.
Sliding down the banister rail.
It's just like sliding down a real slide.
He climbs the stairs, sits on the
banister rail and whoosh!
Off he goes, right down to the
bottom. Duck joins in the game,
too. Bert sits him on the banister
rail, gives him a push and off he
goes too. Just like Bert. Bert and
Duck love their new game and
play it all day.

November 7

Moving

Frank Duckling is moving. He doesn't want to. He likes living here and he
has lots of friends. When they arrive at the new house, Frank looks a bit gloomy.
There is a pond right next to his new house. A pond where lots of ducklings are
playing. Frank goes over to them. He soon makes friends. Frank doesn't mind so
much anymore that he had to move.

The rocking chair

Tamara likes staying at
Grandpa and Grandma's
house. Grandpa and Grandma
have a big rocking chair.
When you sit in it you can
rock to and fro. Tamara is
sitting in the rocking chair
with Duck on her lap.
They are a bit tired after a
whole day's playing. Tamara
and Duck rock gently back
and forth. Ssh!
Tamara is so tired she has
rocked herself to sleep.
Night night, Tamara.
Night night, Duck.

November 9

Grandma is ill

Eric Duckling's grandma is ill. She has the flu. Eric and his mother go to visit her.
Eric takes Grandma a big bunch of flowers and a bag of duckweed. Duckweed
is very good for sick ducks. He's sure Grandma will be pleased with the
flowers and the duckweed. She's sure to get better soon too, now that
she has such lovely flowers to look at and delicious duckweed to eat.

Making a lantern

At Barry's school they are doing something very nice today. They are making lanterns.
Real lanterns with lights inside. First everyone is given a pumpkin. They have to hollow
out the inside, then cut a mouth and two eyes. Then the teacher sticks on a beak made
of orange paper. The pumpkin is a duck! The lantern is nearly finished. It just needs a
candle inside. The light from the candle shines out through the eyes, beak and mouth.
It looks lovely, just as if the lantern duck is smiling.
Barry is very proud of his lantern.

November 11

Three ducklings

Three ducklings with a lantern,
Walking in a row.
What are they doing?
Don't you know?

They're ringing doorbells
And singing a song.
They get candy for singing
As they walk along.

The duck in the puppet theater

Barry's teacher has decided to get the puppet theater out and give the children a show.
All the children in the class are sitting in a big circle. The curtains open.
Up pop a duck and a cat. The cat tries to catch the duck. It's very exciting.
The duck escapes just in time, and the play has a happy ending.
At the end, the duck and the cat make friends.
All the children clap when it is finished.
It was the best puppet show they had ever seen.

November 13

Which animal is it?

A duckling is walking across a field. It is
a very small duckling and doesn't know
very much yet. Suddenly it notices four
tree trunks standing nearby. Or at least
they look a bit like tree trunks. They
look even more like the legs of an animal.
Then the duckling hears a noise: "Moo."
The duckling looks up. There is a large
body attached to the four legs.
The duckling doesn't quite know which
animal it is. It is only a very small
duckling, after all. Do you, perhaps,
know which animal it could be?

207

November 14

Making pancakes

They are having a party today at Hoppy Duckling's house. Father Duck is making pancakes. He has made a big bowl of batter. He takes a big spoonful and pours it into a frying pan. He lets it cook for a while, then can you guess what he does? He tosses it high into the air, then catches it with the other side down, in the pan.
One time it went wrong. Father tossed the pancake so high that it stuck to the ceiling. We'd better not tell Mother Duck. Ssh!

November 15

His own scarf

Victor Duckling is sitting on the sofa. Do you know what he is doing? He is knitting a scarf. Grandma taught him how to knit. Victor can't knit as quickly as Grandma, but that doesn't matter. It's still a long time until winter. Then he will be able to wear the scarf he has knitted himself. It will keep him nice and warm. Even if it snows and freezes, Victor will be snug and cozy in his very own scarf.

A stubborn duckling

Somewhere there is a duckling,
A duckling called Gerry.
Sometimes he's annoying,
And sometimes stubborn. Very.

He won't even listen
To what he is told.
He wants to do it all himself.
He's really far too bold.

November 17

Not for ducklings

Gerard Duckling is in the living room
with Grandpa. Grandpa is smoking a
pipe. "May I try?" asks Gerard.
"Hmm," rumbles Grandpa, "pipes are not
for ducklings." Then Grandpa goes out
of the room for a minute. He leaves his
pipe in the ashtray. A wisp of smoke is
still coming out of the pipe. Gerard
picks it up and sucks. Yuck, how nasty!
It makes Gerard cough horribly.
Grandpa was right. Pipe smoking is not
for ducklings. Gerard thinks that pipe
smoking is not a good thing for
grown-up ducks either!

A real ghost?

Mandy Duckling is playing up in the attic. Suddenly she hears a noise.
"Woo-hoo," goes the noise. Then Mandy sees a white ghost. She jumps with fright.
But then she notices two feet sticking out under the white sheet. She pulls the sheet
away and yes, you've guessed who it is. Freddy!
Joker Freddy wanted to give her a fright, but he didn't really. Well, Mandy was a little
bit afraid, but she's not telling Freddy. Don't you tell him either!

November 19

A delicious present

It is Irene Duckling's mother's birthday
today. Irene and her sister Helen are
making breakfast for Mother. They
make some tea and toast, and pour a
glass of orange juice. Then Irene and
Helen take the breakfast up to Mother in
bed. What a lovely birthday present!
Now Mother can stay in bed that little
bit longer. She's enjoying
her birthday already.

Do you know?

A duckling is sitting looking out of the window. He is sitting very quietly. He would love so much to go outside! He would like to be able to go for a walk, or a swim, or even to fly. That's what all the birds outside do all the time. He can hear them quacking and understands every word they say to each other.

He just doesn't understand why he cannot go outside! The birds outside look a bit different from him, he agrees. He takes a good look at himself. He is fluffy while they are smoother and a different color. They probably aren't ducks, he thinks. Or isn't he a real duck? He has a friend who likes to cuddle him. The ducks outside haven't. What sort of a duck is he really? Do you know?

November 21

Elf houses

Derek and Kooky Duckling are out for a walk in the wood. "Hey, look," says Derek suddenly, "there are some toadstools. Do you think elves live in them?" "Perhaps," says Kooky, "let's look." They lie down on the ground together. They watch and they wait. Perhaps a tiny door will open and an elf will come out. Time passes and they still haven't seen any elves. They get up again. "I don't think any elves live in there," says Derek. "No, neither do I," says Kooky, and they go on with their walk. What a silly pair of ducklings! Do they really think that the elves will come out while they are watching?

November 22

The speedy duckling

I know a duckling
Who comes from Belfast.
This special duckling
Can swim very fast.

Sometimes he races
With friends, just for fun.
But whatever happens,
Belfast Duckling has won!

November 23

Looking for the glasses

Simon Duckling is out for a walk. He meets Digger the mole.
"Good morning, Digger," says Simon. "How are you?"
"Unhappy," says Digger.
"Why, what's the matter?" asks Simon.
"Well," says Digger, "I've lost my glasses. And without my glasses I can't see anything. I can't even see to dig."
"Wait a minute," says Simon, "I'll help you look for them." In no time Simon has found the glasses and gives them to Digger. "Oh, what a relief!" says Digger. "Now I can see again." He disappears underground to go on digging. Simon thinks he might have said thank you, but perhaps moles have other things on their minds.

A squirrel

Mary and Waddle Duckling are walking through the wood. Suddenly something swooshes along a branch of a tree. It is a small, brown animal with a lovely, fluffy tail. It has something in its mouth.

"Look, a squirrel," says Waddle. "Where do you think it's going?"

"To its hole in the tree, of course," says Mary.

"What is it doing?" asks Waddle.

"It is collecting food," says Mary, "because when there is snow on the ground in the winter, the squirrel won't be able to find anything to eat. So it's collecting lots of food now and putting it in its hole. When winter comes it won't need to go in search of food. It can stay in its nice, warm hole and go to sleep."

The ducks don't need to collect food for the winter because the people who live near the duck pond bring bread for them every day. Waddle is relieved. He wouldn't have the first idea of how to go about collecting food for the winter!

The duck shower curtain

At Lisa's house they have a shower curtain. It is there to stop the whole bathroom getting splashed with water when someone takes a shower. The curtain is covered with ducks. All different-colored ducks. And some are bigger than others. So when Lisa is in the shower, she is not alone. She has a shower along with a whole flock of ducks.
Lisa thinks that's fun. So do the ducks.
Well, ducks like water, don't they?

November 26

On Father's back

"May I have a piggyback ride?" Melvin asks his father. "Just this once, because I really, really like it and I'm a bit tired? And I want to play cowboys? Please!"
"Oh, all right," says Father. He gets down on his hands and knees. Melvin puts Duck on Father's back first, then clambers on himself. Father crawls around the room. It looks as if Melvin and Duck are riding a pony. They ride around the room until the pony is tired.
Do you think Melvin will give him a sugar lump?

November 27

A joke, or what?

"Grandpa," says Pip Duckling, "where do
baby ducks come from?"
Grandpa thinks before answering.
Then he says: "Far away, deep in the wood,
is a large lake. Next to this lake is a tall tree.
In the spring, buds appear on this tree.
In the autumn, tiny ducklings
come out of the buds."
Pip looks surprised. Grandpa is
laughing a little bit. Is Grandpa
joking or telling the truth?

November 28

Chewing gum

There was a duckling,
Lived in Belgium.
Very often
He chewed gum.

Blew big bubbles,
Really big ones.
Burst in his face.
Now he's covered in gum!

216

November 29

Funny faces

Mandy and Freddy Duckling are laughing fit to burst. Do you know what they are doing? They are making faces at each other. Freddy is sticking his tongue out and Mandy looks cross-eyed. Then they think of something else. They laugh so much that they get a tummy ache. They roll around on the floor with laughter. Mother Duck, who has just come into the room, doesn't understand why they are laughing so much. Well, she didn't see their funny faces, did she?

November 30

Play-Doh ducks

Robbie is sitting at the table. He is modeling ducks from Play-Doh. He has already made Father Duck and Mother Duck. He's making a small duck now. He gets a small ball of Play-Doh and makes it into a body. Then he makes a head, a beak, and two small legs. When it is finished, Robbie puts it next to Mother and Father Duck.
Oh dear, the little duck has fallen over. Robbie needs to make the feet a bit flatter.
There, the duckling stands proudly next to the big ducks.
What a lovely family of ducks!

December 1

Disco!

Mandy and Freddy Duckling are sitting on the sofa. They are a bit bored.
It is horrible weather so they can't go outside to play.
"I know what we can do," says Freddy suddenly. "Let's make a disco."
"A disco?" says Mandy, "what's that?"
"Well," says Freddy, "you can dance at a disco. It's quite dark and they have
flashing lights. If you close the curtains, I'll put the music on."
Mandy closes the curtains and Freddy turns the lights off. All except one small
table lamp. You can hardly see anything, it's so dark.
Mandy and Freddy dance to the music. Every now and again, Freddy flashes
the lights on and off. It's very nearly like a real disco.

December 2

In the bus

Karl is going shopping in town with Mother. Duck is going too. All three of them are going on the bus, because it is too far to walk. Mother buys the tickets and Karl finds a seat. Karl likes to sit right at the back of the bus. It bounces up and down at the back, and you can see who's driving behind. Karl and Duck would like to stay in the bus all day, driving all around the town. It's a fine idea, but how would Mother ever get her shopping done?

December 3

A new cuddly duck?

Duck is in town with his friend Karl. Karl takes him to a toy shop. Suddenly Duck notices a shelf full of cuddly ducks. There are lots and lots of them and they all look nice and cuddly. Duck, who is also a cuddly duck, feels a little uneasy. Karl wouldn't buy another cuddly duck, would he?
Luckily Karl is just looking. He would never dream of exchanging his own Duck for another. It doesn't matter how beautiful and cuddly they are.

Hibernating

Look at him,
The yawning duck.
He wants to sleep.
No such luck.

Now it's winter.
The snow is great.
But Duck says:
"I will hibernate."

December 5

Where is the hedgehog?

A hedgehog visits Marion Duckling's
garden nearly every day. But Marion
hasn't seen the hedgehog for quite a while.
She is a bit worried.
"Mother," says Marion, "do you know
where the hedgehog has gone?"
"Not exactly," replies Mother, "but I do
know this: hedgehogs hibernate in the
winter. They find a warm place and go
to sleep. When spring comes, all the
hedgehogs wake up again."
Marion thinks it is rather strange,
but she isn't worried anymore.
She hopes that the hedgehog is
having a good sleep.

221

December 6

A new winter coat

Daniel Duckling has a new coat, a lovely and warm winter coat. The old coat didn't fit him anymore. It was much too small. Daniel has grown a lot. The sleeves only reached to his elbows, and the coat only came down to his belly button! A coat like that is fine in the summer, but no good at all in the winter. It would be far too cold. So Daniel got a new coat. He is very proud of it and shows it to everyone.

December 7

Wing muffs

It is getting colder and colder outside. Winter is coming. When it is really cold, it is best to wear gloves. Francis Duckling would like a pair of gloves, but they don't fit on his wings.
Francis's mother thinks of something. She knits him some nice, big wing muffs. They fit exactly on Francis's wings. Mother helps him put them on. Ooh, they're lovely and warm, and they don't fall off. Thank you, Mother Duck!

December 8

Frozen water

Wobble Duckling gets up very early. He feels like taking an early dip in the pond. He walks down to the pond. Just as he is about to dive into the water, he notices that it looks different from usual. It's gotten hard. It is so cold outside that everything is frozen, so the water has turned into ice. Wobble had better go skating instead of swimming. He can have great fun sliding on the ice.

December 9

Skating on the ice

It has frozen hard overnight. The duck pond is covered with ice. Lots of ducks are skating around the pond. Some ducks aren't very good at skating. After only one circle around the pond, they stop for a rest and a chat. A crowd of ducks gathers to talk to each other. The ice begins to crack dangerously. There are too many ducks in one place and the ice can't take the weight.
Quickly they skate away to different parts of the pond. They were just in time – otherwise they would all have gone through the ice!

December 10

A strange story

I once heard tell of a very odd duck,
A duck with seven ears.
I asked the duck why this was so.
He said: "Quite frankly, I don't know,
But it's very much easier to hear."
Seven hands, not two, he also had.
Again, when asked why, he said: "Lad,
One hand to scratch each ear!"

December 11

A den in the house

Tim and Tom Duckling are building a den.
Not outside in the garden, but inside in the
living room. It is far too cold outside.
They put two chairs and the sofa together.
Then they throw a sheet over them to make
a roof. They use another sheet for
the walls. It's just like a nice little house.
When they have finished building, Mother
brings them a glass of lemonade. Tim and
Tom drink their lemonade in their new
den. Mmm, delicious, especially
after all that hard work.

December 12

Footprints in the snow

When Philip Duckling wakes up in the morning, it has been snowing. Everything
has turned white. The trees, the grass…everything is as white as…as snow!
It looks beautiful. Philip goes outside into the garden. The snow creaks underfoot.
You can see where he has walked. Birds have been walking on the snow in the garden
too. You can see their footprints. And rabbit's footprints. They are all different,
but you can easily tell whose they are.

December 13

A duck from Ryde

There once was a duck
Who lived in Ryde.
This silly duckling
Just stayed inside.

He never went anywhere.
He never went out.
If you asked him why,
He said: "I'm tired beyond a doubt."

225

A special bike

Timothy has a very special bike. It doesn't have two wheels or even four wheels.
It has three. So it is called a three-wheeler, a tricycle. One wheel is at the front, the
other two are at the back. But that's not all. Between the back wheels is a luggage
rack. Just the right size for Duck.

When Timothy goes riding, he takes Duck with him. Duck prefers to sit facing
backward. He gets a good view of everything that way. Some other children are a bit
jealous of Timothy. They would like to have a tricycle like his. The other cuddly
ducks are a bit jealous, too. They would love a ride on a tricycle.

Itchy!

Carolyn has been given a lovely sweater. It has a picture of a yellow duck on it. It has twinkly eyes and an orange beak. Carolyn's grandma knitted the sweater. Carolyn loved the sweater, but when she put it on…it was so itchy! Carolyn didn't like it at all. She has to scratch all the time when she is wearing the sweater. She scratches her arms, her tummy, and her neck. The sweater just itches everywhere. Carolyn is very sad. Luckily Grandma has a good idea. She knits Carolyn another sweater, just like the first one, but out of a different wool. Wool that doesn't itch. Isn't Carolyn lucky to have a lovely duck sweater and a Grandma who doesn't mind knitting it twice!

December 16

A red nose

"Atchoo, atchoo," goes Willy. Willy keeps on sneezing because he has a cold. He keeps on blowing his nose in a handkerchief too. Willy has blown his nose so often that it has turned red. His cuddly duck giggles when he sees Willy's red nose. It does look so funny. He may well laugh, but just wait until he gets a cold. He won't be laughing quite so much then. But do you think cuddly ducks get colds? I don't know.

Frost flowers

It has frozen hard overnight. Keith Duckling goes to look through the window to see if the pond has frozen over. But what's this? There is ice on the window! Keith can't see through the window for the ice. And it isn't just plain ice, there are patterns in it. The patterns look rather like flowers. Frost flowers!

December 18

The naughty duckling

I tell of a duck
Who lived in Baghdad.
He was awful, and dreadful,
And naughty, quite bad.

Until one day his father
Said: "Start being good,
Or you'll get a smacked bottom."
Duck stopped where he stood.

The talking-to helped.
He was good now, not bad.
He became awfully good,
Quite the best in Baghdad.

December 19

Nice and warm

Jasper has been playing outside. When he was asleep, it snowed heavily, so when he woke up, there was a thick layer of snow on everything. Jasper went outside and made a big snowman with his friends. When the snowman was finished, they had a snowball fight. Then they built a den from snow. All that playing made Jasper tired. And cold. That's why he's sitting with a blanket over him next to a radiator. Gertie, his cuddly duck, is sitting next to him. Mother has made a big mug of hot chocolate milk for Jasper. That's sure to make him nice and warm inside, too, isn't it?

Food after all!

It snowed in the night. Joshua's garden is covered with a thick layer of snow. Two ducks come to visit Joshua's garden. But now they won't be able to find any food under the snow. Joshua had thought of that. For the past few days, Joshua has been saving bits of bread and leftover potato. He has put them in a big bag. When he sees the ducks, Joshua gets the bag, goes outside, and calls the ducks. He throws some of the bread on the snow. Oh, good, the ducks don't have to go hungry after all. Joshua is looking after them.

December 21

A hole in the ice

John and Theo are walking around the pond. The pond is covered with a thick layer of ice. When it just starts to freeze, the ducks can still swim in the water, but they can't swim anymore now. You can't see any water. John and Theo have an idea. They go home and get two big shovels, then make a hole in the ice with them. They do it very carefully so that they don't fall in themselves. At last the hole is big enough. The ducks can swim around again. John and Theo come back every day with their shovels to make sure that the hole stays open.

December 22

Lovely Christmas cards

Anita is sitting at the kitchen table. She is making cards. Christmas cards to send to people. She is sending one to Grandma and Grandpa. And another to her aunt and uncle. And of course she will send one to her friend Tina, who lives in another town.

Anita has made some lovely cards. She has drawn a duck on them. A duck wearing Santa Claus's hat. With snow. On another card she draws a duck wearing skates, and on another a duck with a sleigh. She makes enough to send a lovely card to everyone she knows. Every card has a duck on it and Anita writes "Merry Christmas!" on each one.

December 23

An ice house

There once was a duckling
Who lived in Greenland.
He didn't have a house
Made of bricks, mud or sand.

His house was of ice.
Made by him, I am told.
I don't know what you think,
But I bet it was cold!

The Christmas tree

It is nearly Christmas. Jenny and Eric are very busy. They are decorating the Christmas tree. Jenny is hanging the ornaments in the tree, one on almost every branch. Eric is doing the tinsel. He's being very careful; otherwise the ornaments might fall off. When they have finished, Mother puts the last decoration right on the top of the tree and adds the lights. They are all very pleased with their Christmas tree. It really does look beautiful.

December 25

Gertie in the tree

Today is Christmas Day. Almost everyone has a Christmas tree at home. So does Jasper. Jasper decorated the tree with his mother. There are some chocolate decorations in the tree too. Jasper is allowed one every now and again.
Do you know what Jasper has done? He has put his toy duck Gertie in the tree, too. Gertie sits there very proudly among the ornaments and tinsel. A real Christmas tree duck!

Christmas at the pond

The ducks down by the pond are celebrating Christmas. They have decorated their own tree. The tree is full of decorations, tinsel and candles. All the ducks are sitting in a big circle around the tree. They are singing Christmas carols. The oldest duck tells the story of Christmas. There are also tasty duck snacks to eat. Most of the ducks think Christmas is one of the best days of the year. It's wonderful to sit around the tree together. All the people who pass by the pond are surprised to see the ducks sitting around their Christmas tree. Most people don't know that ducks celebrate Christmas too!

Still a little bit like Christmas

Alan Duckling looks a bit gloomy.
He is sad that Christmas is over.
His mother thinks of something to
make him feel better. There are still
some cakes left, and some chocolate
decorations in the tree. Alan is allowed
one or two. Then Mother tells a
Christmas story. So it is still a little bit
like Christmas. Alan would like it to
be Christmas all the time.

December 28

Lots of snow

It has been snowing heavily. The duck houses by the pond are almost snowed under.
You can hardly see them. Even Hugo's house is almost hidden, and his is the biggest
of all. You can't see the path leading up to the door. Hugo and his father fetch the snow
shovels. They shovel the snow away from the path so that they can get to the door.
Hugo and his father help other ducks clear away the snow. Then all the ducks can get
to their houses again.

A big rocket

There once was a duck
Who searched for a rocket.
He found one, and bought it
With cash from his pocket.

He sat on it, thought,
I will fire it soon.
With a flash, bang, whoosh
He flew to the moon.

December 30

Fireworks

Kenneth and Tom Duckling can't wait until the new year. One night to go. Father always buys fireworks on New Year's Eve, but they are much too dangerous for small ducklings. So Mother has bought some sparklers. Sparklers are like sticks you light with a match and then, as they burn, they give off pretty sparkles. They look beautiful in the dark, lovely gold and silver stars. Kenneth and Tom are allowed to light one sparkler each today. The others are for tomorrow.

December 31

The very last day

The ducks on the pond are very busy. Today is the very last day of the year. When this day ends, so does the year. So everyone celebrates, including the ducks on the pond. They are making tasty duck snacks to eat this evening. Some of the bigger ducks have bought fireworks. They will set them off at midnight exactly. Because that is when the old year ends and the new year begins. At twelve o'clock. Fireworks are lovely to look at. They make pretty colors in the sky, red, yellow, green, silver and gold. They are noisy too. Everyone is allowed to stay up late, even the tiny ones. Nearly all the ducks think New Year's Eve is the best day of the year. Just like most children!

237